I0780233

For the ones who know temptation is sweetest when it's forbidden—thank you for letting me serve you a story that's equal parts sugar and sin.

After all....

WHAT'S CAKE WITHOUT A LITTLE BITE?

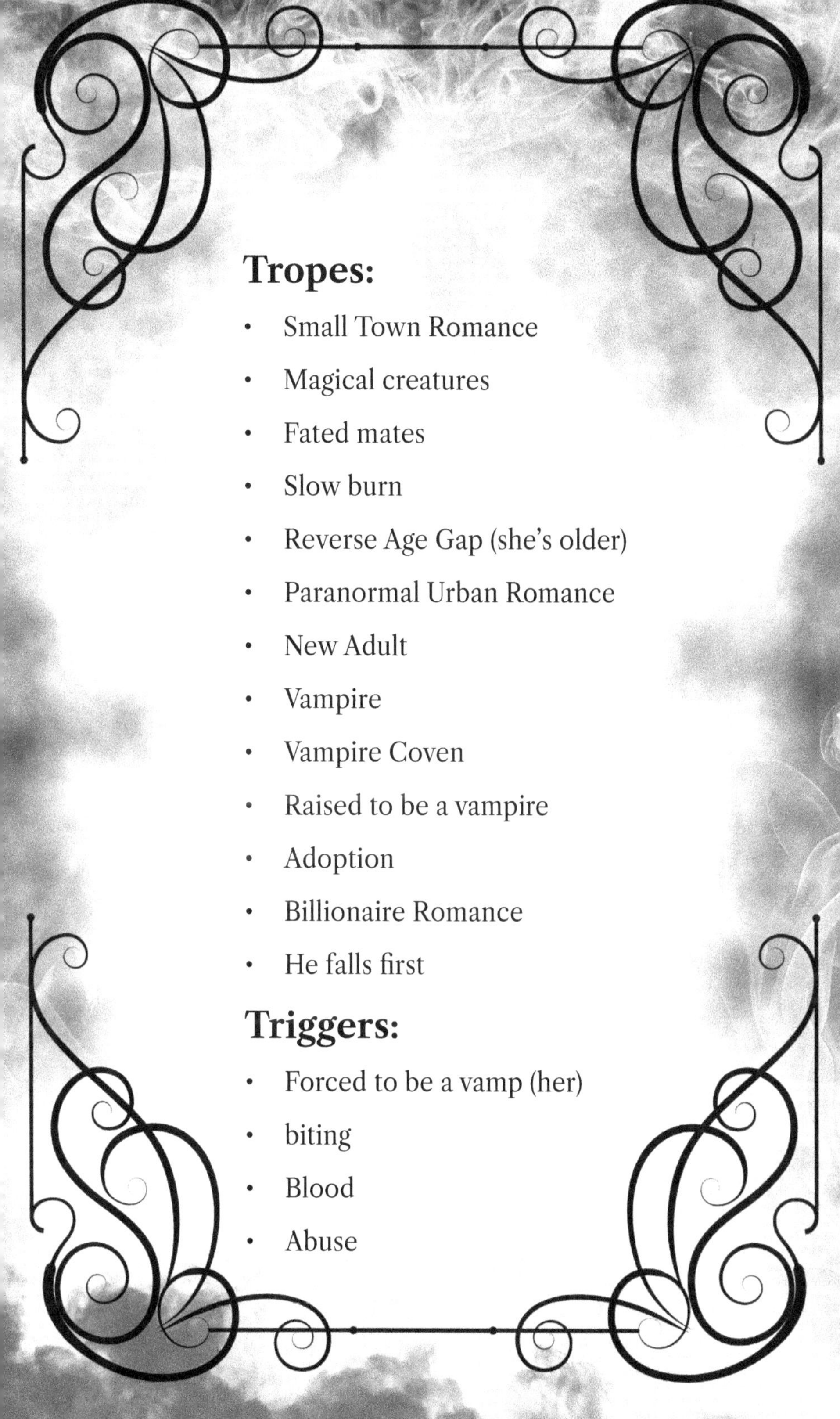

Tropes:

- Small Town Romance
- Magical creatures
- Fated mates
- Slow burn
- Reverse Age Gap (she's older)
- Paranormal Urban Romance
- New Adult
- Vampire
- Vampire Coven
- Raised to be a vampire
- Adoption
- Billionaire Romance
- He falls first

Triggers:

- Forced to be a vamp (her)
- biting
- Blood
- Abuse

Field
Guide

- **Gal-sneaker** - A term from the 1870s meaning "a man devoted to seduction." Chapter 3
- Bit-o-jam - Victorian era slang for "pretty woman". **Chapter 3**
- **Barking at a knot** - A person engaged in an activity that will never bring about the desired result, so it's a waste of time. Used in the 19th century. **Chapter 3**
- **Bow wow mutton** - Sailors used this creative term to refer to really nasty tasting meat. Used in the 19th century. **Chapter 3**
- **Batty-fang** - To thrash thoroughly (a London phrase, though possibly originating from "battre à fin" in French). Used in the 19th century. **Chapter 7**
- **Mouth-pie** - Scolding, usually by a woman. Used in the 19th century. **Chapter 7**
- **Cetus** - In Greek mythology, Cetus is a sea monster often depicted as a giant serpent or whale-like creature. **Chapter 9**
- **La Sorcellerie Élevée** - French for "the elevated witch' **Chapter 26**

Aris

Prologue

$\mathbf{A}$ris Damascus, after years of anticipation, felt a sudden, icy surge of nerves as the velvet darkness of night pressed in on him. He knew this was it, the air crackling with an almost palpable energy: the night of both his death and rebirth. He gazed down at the gift box his parents had left for him, its glossy white surface reflecting the dim lamplight. A cold dread, like icy fingers, gripped him at the thought of opening it; the box felt strangely heavy in his hands. A handwritten card stuck out of the red bow. The card reading 'Happy Birthday and Halloween, Love Mom and Dad' scrolled in his mother's distinctive cursive. Today was his twenty-first birthday.

His hands trembled as he attempted to open it carefully so as not to tear the wrapping paper. Frustrated, he tossed it on his bed and reached underneath, feeling the rough texture of a small wooden box in his grasp. Its worn exterior, weathered by time. With a creak, he lifted the lid, revealing a treasure trove of moments captured in his human life, a life that would soon be gone. His fingers brushed against old photographs; their glossy surfaces cool against his skin. Baby pictures, toddler pictures, even elementary school pictures. Each one a testament to a life lived in the light of day. All pictures from after he was adopted, not a single one from the first month of his life.

He yearned to know his true origins, but all his parents would ever disclose was that they had paid a substantial price for the perfect baby boy. The unanswered questions gnawed at him, leaving him restless and curious. In his youth, he concocted tales about his birth parents, speculating that they were young and were forced to sell him off by his wicked grandparents. Or that they tragically perished in a car accident. Not that he did not cherish his adopted parents; he simply longed to uncover his roots and discover who he truly was, especially before he slipped into the night for all eternity.

Standing up, he sauntered to the open window, the floor creaking beneath his weight. As he gazed out, the mesmerizing sight captivated him. The vibrant rays of the sunset danced across the vast expanse of the sky, casting a breathtaking palette of oranges, reds, and yellows. The magnificent colors appeared to brush away the remnants of the day effortlessly. Taking a deep breath, he inhaled the crisp night air. A profound sense of melancholy washed over him, a bittersweet sadness that tugged at him. He knew that this was the last day he would ever feel the sun's gentle touch upon his skin, forever losing the comforting warmth it provided.

From the ornate chandeliers casting a warm glow to the plush velvet drapes framing the view of the sprawling estate, luxury permeated every corner of his life. He had the opportunity to attend regular schools in Rusthollow, immersing himself in the vibrant world of humans. That way, he would forge connections before his inevitable transformation. They had hoped for him to possess the ability to comprehend and empathize with humans, ensuring they wouldn't be perceived merely as livestock.

The memory of his parents' feeding frenzy flashed before him, a gruesome tableau etched in his mind. He was six, the house quiet in the pre-dawn hush. Drawn by a primal curiosity, he'd crept from his room, the cold wood chilling his bare feet. Peeking through the ornate railing, he witnessed his father's horrifying act: teeth tearing into a woman's flesh. The metallic tang of blood seemed to fill the air. He saw the woman's wide, terrified eyes, reflecting the dim light, then fading as she was led to the floor. The crimson evidence smeared across his father's face, a terrifying mask, sent a jolt of icy fear through Aris. He never spoke of that night, but the lesson was learned: when told to stay in his room at night, he obeyed, the chilling image forever burned into his memory.

However, tonight, everything would change, rendering his past irrelevant. He knew that this would be his last day as a human, and all the doubts were eating at him as he faced the extent of what tonight truly meant.

Weave Your Dreams, Brew Your Magic in

Rusthollow

Aris

Chapter 1

Four months ago

The warmth of the sun kissed Aris's face from the window as he stared out it, a fleeting pleasure as he knew these sunlit days were dwindling for him. Had he truly made the most of them within the sterile walls of college? His forest green eyes, usually bright, now seemed distant, lost in thought. The faint scent of old paper and floor wax filled the air as he pondered the practicality of his hard-earned education. Four years, marked by the rustle of turning pages and the murmur of lectures, were culminating today, his final class done. With a soft thud, Aris closed his heavy hematologic care book, the smooth cover cool beneath his fingertips.

"Mr. Damascus, can you please stay after?" Professor Virgil Grimbald's voice echoed, snapping him to attention. The professor's brown hair, styled like a monk's tonsure, was thinning on top. Aris guessed he was around fifty, his face lined with age and noticed the way his tweed coat button strained slightly around his middle.

Aris watched with heavy eyes as the last

of the students noisily scraped their chairs and filed out, the echo of their chatter fading into the hallway. A profound sense of loss like a cold weight in his chest, filled him. Curiosity, a fluttering anticipation, tickled his stomach. He had a feeling he knew what the old warlock was going to lecture him on again, the familiar drone already ringing in his ears, but he wasn't sure what his answer would be this time if pressed to tell the truth. His heart warred, a frantic bird beating against his ribs, with a decision that had seemed out of his hands his entire life.

He looked up, meeting those gentle, muddied brown eyes. "What is it, Prof?"

"I just wanted to remind you it is not too late," Virgil murmured. He placed his freckled hand, warm and slightly rough, on top of Aris's, a silent offering of comfort. Aris could feel the slight pressure, a grounding sensation in the swirling unease whirling through him.

"I know," Aris sighed. He knew his parents would never force the issue if he backed out. Yet, the internal struggle—a relentless storm of wanting to be embraced by his family or running and hiding in the noisy world of humans, living the short-lived life of a mortal—was a struggle he fought every day. The battle grew stronger, a painful knot twisting inside his heart with each tick of the clock in the hall, each chime a reminder of the dwindling time he had left to decide. "I am going to be fine."

"I just want to make sure you know you have a choice." His voice was a low murmur that barely cut through the heavy silence. The worry in Virgil's eyes shone, a tangible thing like a physical weight pressing down.

Laughing, Aris stood up. Shaking his head, he said, "I know I have a choice, and I know what I am doing. Thanks for the concern. You're a good man,

Prof. Never forget that. I hope you have a nice summer break." He shoved his class book into his backpack.

"Alright," Virgil nodded. "I hope you have a nice summer break, and I would love to see you around again. Don't be a stranger and come by, even just to say hi."

Aris beamed, waving a last goodbye as he departed. The door clicked shut behind him. Stepping outside, he waved off the human chauffeur. The car, paid for by his parents, gleamed under the afternoon sun. He craved the solitude of a walk, the pavement solid beneath his feet, hoping to quell the unease gnawing at him. School was out; it was time to plot his transition. A cold knot twisted in his stomach. *Could I truly handle this?* The stories of the unbearable pain echoed in his mind. Yet, he knew he'd fulfill his duty. He just needed to bury the fear and uncertainty clawing at his soul, to find the resolve to face the ordeal ahead.

Walking off campus, he wasn't sure where he was heading, just that he wanted to escape. Looking over his shoulder, he saw the chauffeur trailing him, a nondescript male, much like the several before him. The crunch of his shoes on the gravel path was the only sound besides the rustle of leaves. They never seemed to last long, so he never bothered to learn their names. The sun beat down on his tanned skin, warming him with a golden glow, while a cool breeze brushed his face, carrying the scent of drying leaves. The trees were transforming, their leaves turning from vibrant green to shades of fiery orange.

Inhaling, he smelled something delicious—an aroma that tickled his senses. Turning, he saw Magickal Morsels, a witchy bakery that served spelled treats. The cozy brick building stood bathed in the warm afternoon light, its large picture windows showcasing a dazzling array of enchanted sweets. Peppermint swirls shimmered; chocolate confections pulsed with a faint, magical hum. A sugary aroma wafted out as the door opened, and a chime softly rang.

The bakery was a familiar reward; a place he'd visited countless times. He vividly recalled his first visit with Amara, his adopted mother. Amara had asked him what treat he desired, and he'd eagerly chosen a Gigga-mon Roll. He could almost taste the sugary sweetness and feel the ticklish laughter spell taking hold. The bakery's interior was still the same: the worn wooden counters gleamed under the warm lights. The only difference was the witch behind the counter, who appeared to be a college student; a pretty, bubbly blonde, with a bright smile.

"Welcome to Magickal Morsels," her sweet voice chirped. "Are you looking for anything in particular?"

Golden sunlight spilled through the picture window, washing the room in a soft, buttery glow. Glass cases shimmered, displaying a vibrant array of pastries and treats in countless colors and sizes. The air hummed with a sweet, warm fragrance of spices; the sharp tang of cloves danced with the comforting scents of cinnamon and vanilla. Bookshelves lined the walls, adorned with glass herb jars and other small curios.

"I don't know if you still have it," he paused, ruffling his hair. The thought of asking for a treat, a sugary relic of childhood, made his cheeks flush with a warmth that felt almost childish. "But you guys used to have this cinnamon roll that made you giggle."

"Oh, we have a fresh batch over here." Her voice, a warm invitation, drew him in. She rounded the corner behind the gleaming counter. With a gentle slide, she opened the glass door, releasing a rush of warm, sweet cinnamon into the air. She carefully extracted a cinnamon bun nestled snugly in a quaint little parchment paper wrap, its edges slightly browned and glistening. "This is the Giggamon Bun you are talking about."

"Perfect, I'll take one."

"Let me put it in a box, and I'll ring you up." Her bright blue eyes sparkled.

"Thank you," he said, looking around. The chauffeur stood just outside the door, a silent sentinel, his gaze unwavering, tracking every flicker of movement. Aris's eyes, sharp and focused, darted to her name tag, the light glinting off the plastic. "Alita."

He paid for the warm, yeasty bun, the scent of cinnamon clinging to it, then stepped out into the bright, crisp air. As he strolled, he devoured the Giggamon Bun, the soft dough melting in his mouth. He felt a tingle the instant the spell took hold, and a joyous storm of giggles erupted, echoing in the street. Vivid memories, a warm kaleidoscope of his mother bringing him here, flashed through his mind as he savored the last bite. One final burst of giggles bubbled out, making him feel buoyant and lighthearted.

He pivoted; the leather of his expensive shoes whispering against the cobblestones and fixed his gaze on the chauffeur. The man stood stiffly, his face a blank mask. "You can go get the car. I'll be at EnchanTea grabbing a drink."

The bell above the door jingled merrily as he stepped into the charming little cafe. His eyes fell upon several vintage wooden tables, their metal spindle legs glinting softly in the warm light. The long, scarred vintage bar top gleamed, behind which stood the barista. The scent of roasted coffee beans hung heavy in the air. Her auburn hair was piled high in a bun, a few stray strands framing a face that held a warm greeting in its blue eyes.

"Hey, Lily," he said, glancing up at the laminated menu, its colors slightly faded under the warm lighting. The murmur of other patrons buzzed behind him, a low hum of conversation and clinking silverware that filled the cozy space as he debated between the daily specials. "Can I get a Clarity Tea Latte, please?"

"You got it," Lily smiled as she rang up his order.

He lowered himself into the creaking wooden chair at the table, leaning back against its worn surface. Barely a minute passed before she arrived, placing the steaming tea on the table with a gentle clink. He inhaled deeply; the delicate rose petals mingling with the earthy scent of the spices. The first sip was mildly sweet, an earthy warmth spreading through him. He held the warm ceramic cup, feeling the soothing heat radiating into his hands. Through the clear plate-glass window, he watched crimson and gold autumn leaves dance on the crisp breeze as the sleek limo silently approached and stopped in front of the cafe.

Walking into the house, the only natural light, a warm, golden ray, streamed in from the open doorway, quickly fading to near black as he shut the heavy door with a soft thud. He walked into the kitchen, where the bright, clinical overhead lighting buzzed softly, illuminating every corner of the windowless room when he flicked the switch on. The dark wood cupboards, cool to the touch, and the sleek, white marble counters gleamed under the bright lights. The sharp, citrusy scent of cleaning solution hung heavy in the air, a clean but artificial aroma.

A soft cough echoed from the hallway. Leaving the kitchen, he walked towards the sound. In the dim hallway, shadows danced on the walls, barely illuminated by the faint light filtering from the doorway. He saw his mother, Amara, standing there. He strained to see the features of her pixie-shaped face, only just making out the blue of her eyes in the gloom. The outline of her blonde hair, pulled back into a chignon, was a pale halo in the darkness.

"How was your last day of school, my handsome baby lambkin?" Her sweet voice lilted, a melody that shimmered like sunlight on water.

"It was fine, Mom," Aris said stoically.

"Will you miss it?" she murmured softly.

"Miss what?" His brow furrowed, casting a shadow over his green eyes.

"School and all your day friends."

"I'll be fine." He shrugged. *How can I explain to her I stopped trying to make friends knowing I wouldn't be able to be around them after the turning?* "Plus, I'm happy school's out. I have more free time to drive you crazy now." A playful wink accompanied his words as he leaned casually on the doorjamb.

"As if you haven't been succeeding at that your entire life," she laughed. "Do I smell cinnamon?"

Chuckling, he shook his head. "I stopped at Magickal Morsels and took a walk down memory lane."

"Oh?"

"Yes," he said, running a hand through his tou-

sled hair. "Remember those nights when I was little, and you took me there?"

"Of course, I do. I may be one-hundred and eighty-nine years old, but I am not senile, my baby lambkin," she snorted.

"You are kind of creeping up there in years now that you mention it," he smirked. "And I swear there are some grey streaks in your—"

"Don't you dare finish that sentence!" Amara stepped into the dim light streaming from the kitchen. The soft illumination seemed to highlight the delicate texture of her porcelain skin, making her appear almost fragile. Even after well over a century, she still looked twenty-four years old, her youthful beauty defying time. A slight pout played on her lips, causing her slightly elongated fangs to glisten like dewdrops. "Do you really think I look old?"

"No, Mom," he grumbled. He rolled his eyes, the whites flashing. "I was teasing you, and you know it. You look exactly as you did the day you were turned."

"You, my lambkin, are shameful!" She swiped at his chest playfully. "Now we have more serious things to discuss."

"Ughh," he groaned. "Do we have to?"

"Yes," she sighed, the sound like a soft breeze rustling through leaves, reaching over to smooth out the worn cotton of his t-shirt. "You really should not dress like such a slob! You have an allowance that affords you such niceties, and you chose to wear a shirt with holes in it."

"Your idea of a serious conversation is you belittling my clothing choices?"

"That's not what I meant," she snorted. "And you know it. I mean, as a Damascus, you need to present yourself in a certain light. Our coven looks upon us as leaders. So, we need to present ourselves as respectable and—"

"I was just in the light," he interjected. "Everyone dresses like me. Not like a Victorian princess."

"Was that another age joke?"

"If you want to call it that." A smirk, a silent, visual taunt.

"You are an incorrigible rascal and should be ashamed of poking fun at your mother like that."

"What if I said I love you? Then will you stop trying to dress me as if we still live in the 1800s?"

"Hmph," she exhaled. "We have gotten off topic." She shook her head, wisps of hair swirling. "We have the party planner coming tonight to plan the ball for your twenty-first birthday. I want you to rest up so you are not so... grumpy. Dress presentable."

"Great planning a party to drain me of blood sounds fun." He laughed sardonically, the sound echoing hollowly in the high-ceilinged hall. He brushed past his mother, the faint scent of her floral perfume momentarily filling his nostrils, and started towards the grand, shadowed staircase, each step creaking softly under his weight.

"It is our tradition, a ceremony representing transition from life to—" she started the familiar lecture.

"To my afterlife" he cheered, the words ringing hollow. "Yeah, me."

"You will not talk with that level of sass tonight,"

she said sternly.

"Yes, ma'am." He saluted her.

A heavy sigh escaped her lips, and she slowly shook her head. "Wear a suit. Your father and I spent an arm and a leg for you to look presentable. Holey jeans and a band shirt are not presentable."

Johnna Dee

Magickal Morsels Bakery

Harlow

Chapter 2

Harlow Rathmore felt the sticky warmth of blood tracing a path down her chest, a gruesome stain. An icy fist of fear clenched her gut. The rundown house was a cavern of absolute darkness, smelling of dust and decay, as she clutched the throbbing wound in her left shoulder. Her grey dress, once soft against her skin, was now heavy and soaked crimson. Footsteps echoed closer, each one a hammer blow in the suffocating silence. Her heart thundered a frantic rhythm, threatening to crack her ribs. Her head spun, the edges of her vision speckled with dancing black spots.

She stumbled, her foot catching on an uneven floorboard, and fell against the rough stone wall. A dull thud echoed in the sudden silence, and she felt her bones rattle with the jarring impact, a wave of sharp pain blooming in her right shoulder.

"Lo-lo," a menacing voice said in a singsong tone. "Do you really think you can run from me?"

Tears streamed down her face, blurring her vision as she pushed away from the rough plaster of the wall. The thumping bass of Blues Hex, the local jazz band she had desperately wanted to hear to escape Clark, was now a distant memory, replaced by the metallic tang of blood that hung in the air. Never had she imagined it would end with the lead singer's teeth sinking into her flesh, a primal attempt to kill her. His heavy footsteps echoed closer, each thud a hammer blow to her fading consciousness. She stumbled into the dimly lit kitchen. The linoleum did nothing to muffle her footsteps as she yanked open a drawer, the clatter of silverware a desperate symphony as she searched for a weapon.

"There you are, Lo-lo," he whispered.

Harlow woke with a start, a gasp escaping her lips. The lingering images of the nightmare flickered behind her eyelids, her breathing ragged and shallow. Her pulse hammered in her ears, a frantic drumbeat as she fought to convince herself it was over—just a nightmare. Wide, panicked hazel eyes darted around the dimly lit room, searching for the familiar. Trembling hands smoothed strands of tousled, chocolate-brown hair. Rubbing her throbbing temples, she could almost feel the residual fear clinging to her skin like a cold sweat. The soft cotton of the sheets offered little comfort as she climbed out of bed, the cool air raising goosebumps on her arms. Sleep was a distant shore she couldn't reach, the nightmare's echoes still too loud in the quiet room.

The darkened bedroom was a world of hushed shadows. She gazed around, eyes adjusting to the gloom, the film she'd painstakingly applied to the window, bit of daylight. The muted blue curtains, soft as a whisper, were drawn closed. She could almost feel the faint heat radiating through them, a reminder of the sun's thwarted power. They wouldn't be able to block out the light if it were not for the film, but they were pretty and her favorite color. The faint digital glow of the clock on her bedside table illuminated the time, a stark reminder that stepping outside was an impossibility.

She grabbed her navy-blue sheets, the soft cotton cool against her skin, and her blanket as she made the bed, the crisp scent of lavender rising from the fabric. Smoothing them out, she turned to leave the room. She walked into her living room. The antique floral sofa she had picked up twenty years ago looked like it was wearing thin in spots. Grabbing the TV remote, she turned it on. The fifteen-year-old TV flickered, filling the room with a pale light. She rested her heels on the smooth, dark wood of the coffee table that had traveled with her for the last fifty years. Flipping through the channels until she found a detective show, the sounds of sirens and hushed voices filled the air. As she got lost in the flashes of images on the grainy screen, she felt her muscles relax and the nightmare fade from the front of her thoughts.

Harlow smoothed her crisp white business suit, the cool fabric rustling against her skin, and adjusted her blue silk shirt. The soft material felt luxurious against her skin. Her chocolate-brown hair, pulled back into a low bun, gleamed under the soft lights. A quick spritz of lilac perfume filled the air with a delicate floral scent as it landed on her ivory skin. She smoothed a shimmery gloss across her rose-red lips, and the subtle fragrance mingled with the lilac. Light touches of blush added a warm flush of color to her pale skin.

She paused, catching her reflection in the antique mirror, its silvered surface cool to the touch as she steadied herself. Her eyes, bloodshot from sleepless nights, scanned for imperfections.

Rusthollow, she thought, a name that tasted like ash on her tongue. Five years. The wind howled outside, rattling the windowpanes, a constant reminder

of her isolation. Six months ago, the whispered words, "stray dog," still echoed in her mind like a dissonant chord as she heard others talking about her behind her back. She remembered the sharp intake of breath, the sting of humiliation. She'd come here seeking solace, a place where life would bloom with friendships, banishing the loneliness of decades of solitary self-isolation. But no matter where she went without a coven, she was adrift, forever an outsider.

"You look fine," she murmured to herself.

She turned from the mirror's reflection; her gaze drifted to the clock. The red numbers glowed: she had thirty minutes until she needed to be there, a fifteen-minute drive. She chewed her lip, debating—linger here in the quiet, or arrive early? Thump-thump-thump, a blur of gray fur, a fleeting shadow, sped past her, the soft pad of paws barely audible on the wooden floor.

"Oh, no you don't," she growled. "Shadow, do not touch me!"

The lykoi cat effortlessly jumped onto the mattress. His golden-brown eyes, narrowed to slits, surveyed her with what seemed like utter boredom from his fuzzy, wolf-like face. The dim light caught the grizzled texture of his dark roan-colored fur, making it look even wilder and untamed.

"Do not let your fur get on my suit!" she grumbled. "I just used the lint roller."

She gazed down at her only friend. For twenty-five years, that friend had listened, answering with nothing more than a soft meow that rumbled like distant thunder. She remembered the metallic clang of the shelter door, the scent of cedar chips and other animals, the first day she saw those tawny eyes gleaming behind the cold bars. She had intended to discuss doves for an event, but instead, she had fallen in love with the magical little creature. Boy did she not know all the complications that would come with this little fur ball.

With a soft sigh that ruffled the quiet air, she reached out. Her fingers, cool against his warm fur, scratched gently behind his ears. A low rumble, a purr vibrating in the air, answered her touch. "I guess I have some kind of coven with you, Shadow. So, I am not as alone as I feel. But I am serious; don't get fur on me."

The door creaked open as she approached, the aged wood groaning a low note. Snatching up the portfolio binder on the oak console table next to the door, its leather cool against her fingertips, she glanced over her shoulder, the rustling of pages a soft whisper as she flipped it open. "I'll be back in a couple of hours; don't wreak havoc on the furniture." Giggling, anticipating the mischief he'd get into, she knew he would behave at least until the moon cast its full, silvery glow across the night sky.

She walked down the path to her faded red pickup truck. The cool metal of the door handle pulled with ease at the door creaked open. Rolling her windows down, she felt the breeze whip through her hair, carrying the scent of damp grass. The moon, a silvery sliver in the inky sky, hung low, casting long shadows as she drove; the hum of the tires against the cracked asphalt accompanied her journey to the outskirts of town.

Her thoughts drifted to the portfolio of designs, the crisp paper whispering promises of the grand party she was planning. A wince tightened her face as the reason clawed at her mind. Vampire laws and traditions were such a murky, mired pool. Even as she envisioned the 'Turning Party' her stomach rolled in knots. The elite leaders of the local vampire coven had raised a child from birth to turn him on his twenty-first birthday. She had never met the Damascus's yet, but with how she was forced into this life, the entire concept made her nauseous. Planning this party, with its music and masks, was bringing back nightmares, their icy grip tightening around her heart, a grip she had thought long gone. But she needed the money, so she was going to take the job. She hoped that this would bring her more clients and maybe she would be considered less of a stray one day. She was tired of moving around, the constant shifting leaving her bones weary, and wanted a home of her own.

The tires crunched on the gravel path as she drove toward the manor house. Announcing herself through the crackling loudspeaker, she kept her gaze fixed on the ornate iron gates. Decorated with two ornate lion heads, their fangs elongated, the doors slowly swung open. She drove toward the grand columned entrance, the house looming into view.

The butler was a rigid figure on the porch, waiting patiently. His dark suit, crisp and immaculate, seemed painted on. His brown hair and eyes did nothing to make his features stand out; he was purposefully nondescript. As she approached, the metallic tang of blood tickled her nose—a scent that screamed "human." Shock washed over her, stark and undeniable, as she wordlessly followed him into the house.

As they stepped into the grand foyer, the scent of dozens of red roses filled the air, their velvety petals a stark contrast to the white vase and dark, antique wood of the table beneath. Cool, smooth white marble met their feet, the sound of their footsteps echoing in the vast space. A grand staircase, a swirling sculpture of carved wood, ascended to the second and third floors, beckoning them upwards. Gleaming white walls stretched, pristine and vast, towards the vaulted ceilings high above, where a crystal chandelier sparkled, and refracted light into a thousand shimmering rainbows.

A soft cough, like the brushing of a tree branch against a wall, caught her attention, and she turned back to the human. With a flick of his wrist, he gestured towards a room on the right side of the hall. She nodded, the click of her heels echoing softly as she moved in that direction. Inside, Amara Damascus sat on the couch, her ankles crossed demurely. Her blonde hair was perfectly coiffed in a tight chignon. The blush-colored silk of her dress flowed to her ankles, complementing her pale skin like a rose against porcelain. Her blue eyes, cool and distant as a winter sky, seemed to look right through her.

The flicker of movement near the fireplace drew her gaze. Her eyes traveled up the form of the male, a sculpted vision of a Greek statue brought to life before her very eyes. He was a tower of a man; muscles defined beneath his clothes. The grey slacks, stretched taut across his powerful legs, spoke of contained strength. His crisp white shirt hugged his broad chest as he crossed his arms, a silent challenge. Finally, her gaze met his, locking onto the deep forest green of his eyes, and she felt herself falling into their shadowed depths. A silent gasp caught in her throat, and the frantic rhythm of her heart echoed in her ears.

"Are your shoelaces tied?" His husky voice, a low rumble that vibrated in the air, drawled as a slow, predatory smile stretched across that sharply defined, triangular jaw, the movement creasing the corners of his eyes. "I don't want you falling too hard for me the way you keep staring?"

Aris

Chapter 3

Aris drank in the sight of the goddess before him, unnoticed. The rich chocolate waves of her hair cascaded over her shoulder with a soft rustle as her hazel eyes swept across the foyer. The crisp white suit molded to her statuesque form, hinting at the curves beneath. Finally, her slow gaze met his, and a spark ignited in those depths. Her eyes, hazel pools that seemed to soften as they held his, told him everything he needed to know.

"Aris Damascus!" Amara scolded, glaring at him before turning her gaze back to the party planner. "Quit being so exasperating. Please ignore my little lambkin. No matter how much I have tried to teach him manners, it never seems to sink in."

"My sweet bit-o-jam don't harp on the boy," Tiberias chastised, walking into the room. "The boy can't help if he's a gal-sneaker."

Aris gazed at his father's dirty blonde hair, meticulously cropped into a crew cut, catching the light. His green eyes, mirroring Aris', sparkled with mirth, tiny wrinkles fanning out from the corners. In the low light, his strong, square jaw showed sharply, a rugged landscape etched against the soft shadows. A wide, inviting smile stretched across his face. A low chuckle rumbled in his chest, a warm, comforting sound as he ambled over. The soft thud of his leather loafers was barely audible on the plush rug as he plopped his five-foot eleven frame down next to Amara.

"I am Tiberias Damascus," Tiberias stated. He gestured towards the plush couch across from him, its velvety damask surface inviting you to sink into its depths. "Please have a seat and show us what you have planned for my boy's big day."

Exhaling deeply, Aris looked around the room. "As long as there's no balloon animals and face painting, I am okay with whatever."

"Aris!" Amara exclaimed.

"You need not worry; there will be none of that," Harlow stated. The appraising stare, a flicker of warm curiosity, vanished. Now, haughty disdain filled those eyes, sharp and glacial, as they fixed upon him. He felt the shift like a sudden drop in temperature.

"Then show us what you've got," Aris smiled slyly, knowing he could win her over.

Harlow opened the heavy leather portfolio, and she began going over the party plans. Aris, lounging nearby, listened more to the sweet, melodic lilt of her voice, a comforting sound like a gentle stream, than the actual words she spoke. Crisp, precise details of the party were unimportant to him. The upcoming event was what his mother wanted. The bright lights, the clinking of champagne glasses, the prestigious guest list—the entire tradition was all his mother's doing. If he had his way, he would get it done swiftly and quietly and be over with it. *Is that what I really want?* The thought floated through his mind as self-doubt crept in.

He banished the tempest of warring emotions, his gaze settling on the sketched images. It was a map of the grand ballroom, with tables meticulously placed like chess pieces. He squinted, trying to lock onto the plans they were discussing as the echoes of their voices floated through the room. His mother's suggestions, a gentle melody, threatened to be drowned out as his thoughts drifted again. A yawn pressed against his lips, a silent wave threatening to break. He raised a hand, hoping to mask the breach of etiquette, but the sharp glint in his mother's eye told him she had witnessed his lapse.

"Do you have any feedback, lambkin?" Amara said, arching a blonde eyebrow.

"I think the plans you have made so far sound great, Mom." Aris's voice was smooth as silk, and a sweet smile bloomed on his face. It was the same smile he used to get what he wanted, a practiced expression that always seemed to melt his mother's resolve. "You have excellent taste, so I always defer to you on these matters."

Amara tilted her chin down, a silent reprimand, while her blue eyes, bright as a summer sky, sparkled with a motherly annoyance.

"Well, this is a great start," Amara said, turning her glance back to Harlow. "Please make the revisions we discussed, and we can meet up again to go over the adjustments." The words echoed slightly in the otherwise silent room as Amara stood with a faint rustle of her skirt, leaving the room without a further word.

"It was a pleasure to meet you," Tiberias said, extending his hand to Harlow.

Harlow accepted his handshake, saying, "I am happy to be working for you and your family."

Tiberias slipped out of the room. Aris, a looming shadow against the fading light, shifted to intercept Harlow, his presence a palpable barrier before she could follow. She paused on the settee and looked up at him, annoyance radiating from every pore.

Aris's voice, a low rumble, cut through the si-

lence of the room. "Let me walk you out, Harlow." He reached out to help her. Her eyes shifted to his outstretched hand.

She brushed away the offered appendage as she stood up. "I can show myself out."

"Or I can show you something else if you'd like," he said, a smirk playing on his lips, his voice a low, husky, breathy sound. He enjoyed watching the flicker of surprise widen her eyes, the pupils dilating like a flower opening to the sun.

Her expression shifted like the sky before a storm, her smooth forehead creasing into a frown as she tilted her head back to gaze at him. A deep furrow etched itself between her brows. His eyes, catching the dim light, were drawn to the rose-red stain of her lips, and the subtle, sharp point of one slightly elongated fang digging into the soft flesh of her lower lip. He lifted his hand, the air cool against his skin, and his thumb gently tugged her bottom lip down, freeing it from the fang's subtle pressure. He felt the soft give of her skin. She held her breath; the silence amplifying the moment.

He grinned, crinkling the corners of his eyes, and leaned in close, his face a breath away from hers. He inhaled deeply, the delicate scent of lilac perfume filling his senses, a sweet floral aroma that hinted at spring. "Wanna go to my room and do some math? We can add a bed, subtract our clothes, divide your legs and multiply." *What perverse impulse made me utter that pathetic line? Was it the cloying lilac perfume, thick in the air that muddied my thoughts? Or perhaps it was the tantalizing glints of gold swirling within the warm depths of her hazel eyes, reflecting the dim light.* More likely, he wanted to test the waters, to pierce through the icy wall she projected, a palpable wave of coolness that stiffened the air between them.

"No," she stated, shoving him away.

Clutching her portfolio tight to her chest, she scampered away. The heavy front door thudded shut behind her with a resounding click that echoed in the sudden silence.

"Aris," a scolding voice called as he walked out into the foyer.

There, at the top of the dimly lit staircase, stood his mother. Her fingers tapped a restless rhythm against her crossed arms.

"Do not flirt with her," Amara reprimanded, shaking her head. "She is not of clean blood; she is a stray. You have a place in this coven of standing. You—"

"Mom," he groaned, rolling his eyes. "I was just teasing. Please don't start."

"There is a hierarchy, and that... that woman. She is nothing but a... a... bow-wow mutton. It would be like barking at a knot trying to be with that woman. You need someone who fits in the life you are destined to lead. That stray woman never will."

"Mom," Aris sighed. "It's really not that serious. So, let's just pause for a moment and take a breath."

"I am being serious," Amara stated, pushing her shoulders back. Her voice, though small, echoed in the vast room, each word a sharp sting on his ears. He felt a familiar shrinking sensation, like when he was a child all over again and was being lectured for eating too much ice cream and throwing up all over the two-hundred-year-old Persian rug. "If you really need a dalliance, you could play with her after turning but remember she is a toy that you should not expect to play with for long."

"You're being so dramatic over a few jokes," he huffed.

"Let me reiterate, and you will pay attention," Amara growled, slamming a fist on the stair rail. "She will not turn you before the ceremony by accident since you went sniffing around that bow-wow mutton. Stay away from her."

"Fine, Mom," Aris mumbled, his brow furrowed in frustrated compliance. He knew, with a heavy feeling in his chest, that not a single word of the lecture he was enduring would penetrate the wall he was already building in his mind. "But could we stop talking like we are still living in the eighteen-eighties?"

Johnna Dee

Damascus

Coven

Harlow

Chapter 4

Harlow walked into the apartment, the door shutting with a soft thud; the sound echoed in the small space. A few feet away, Shadow sat, his tiny frame a dark silhouette against the worn rug. His tail thumped a rapid rhythm against the floor, a soft drumroll of anger. Though he sat still, his eyes blazed with a tawny intensity, and the air fairly vibrated with his barely suppressed energy.

"Well, hello to you too," Harlow sighed. "Are you hungry?"

Shadow tilted his head, his black fur rippling slightly, and his eyes, usually soft amber, now seemed to radiate a furious rage, a burning intensity that felt too big for his small body.

She walked to the kitchen, the linoleum cool beneath her bare feet, the faint scent of lemon cleaner lingering in the air. Flipping the light on, the bright blue walls seemed to glow, reflecting the harsh kitchen lights. The oak cabinets stood solid, contrasting with the cool, smooth feel of the white-tiled counters beneath her fingertips as she glided them across the counter. She had tried to add as much color as she could to make it feel like home with splashes of blue, a vibrant attempt to warm the sterile space.

Reaching into the cupboard, she grabbed a can of tuna cat food. With a soft plop, she emptied its contents into a navy-blue ceramic bowl. Shadow mewed expectantly, his fur rubbing against her slacks.

Walking to his woven mat, she placed the bowl down next to his water dish. Shadow gobbled down the food, the sound of his enthusiastic eating filling the quiet room.

The hum of the refrigerator filled the otherwise silent kitchen as she pulled the door open. A waft of cold air rushed out, carrying with it a metallic tang. Inside, neatly stacked, were bags of blood, each labeled with the Onyx Eclipse Blood Bank logo. These bags, though a far cry from the real thing, were the only barrier between her and the raw, visceral urge to sink her teeth into a warm neck. She grabbed a bag, the cool plastic slick against her skin. It wasn't the most palatable; the preservatives lent a chemical aftertaste, but it kept the beast at bay. With a sigh, she poured the viscous liquid into a glass. Years ago, the taste would have sent shivers down her spine, triggering violent gag reflexes. Now, with practiced ease, she tilted the glass back and gulped it down, the metallic tang coating her tongue with only a slight grimace.

Onyx Eclipse Blood Bank catered for a pretty penny to local vampires. Witches, humans, and other magickal creatures can donate money for a quick buck. She finished the last of her meal and went to her office in the living room. Pulling her notes, she started to adjust the plans according to Mrs. Damascus's orders. Looking up availability and prices for items she requested from Onyx Eclipse Blood Bank catered to the local vampires for a pretty penny. Witches, humans, and other magickal creatures, lured by the promise of a quick buck, could donate blood. Sated, she finished the last of her thick, ruby-red liquid meal, the bitter tang lingering on her tongue. Rising, she padded to her office in the living room; the rug muffling her footsteps. Pulling her dog-eared notes under the cool glow of the desk lamp, she started to adjust the plans according to Mrs. Damascus's precise orders, the paper rustling softly. Her fingers flew across the keyboard, looking up availability and prices for the requested items, the screen's light reflecting in her focused eyes.

Her mind drifted back to the memory of him: alluring green eyes that sparkled like emeralds in sunlight, and muscular arms that she imagined felt strong and warm wrapped around her. She could almost smell the faint, clean scent of his blood. *Why am I even entertaining thoughts of him? He is a cocky, spoiled brat, who is like a hundred years younger than me. A gorgeous, spoiled brat who knows it.* Her mind drifted, the image of his muscular hands a phantom sensation against her skin—a warm, firm pressure she could almost feel. How would they truly feel if they touched her? A blush crept up her neck. With a shake of her head, she scattered the burgeoning thoughts of him like leaves in a gust of wind.

Shadow jumped onto her lap. His weight was a comforting warmth as one hand stroked his fur. The rhythmic rasp of his purring, a soft, vibrating rumble, soothed her nerves as she scrolled through her vendor's website. The screen's cool light illuminated her face as she scanned the crisp, white images of linens.

"I just don't get it, Shadow," she murmured. "It's so... so... so barbaric to raise someone from birth to turn him into a vampire. What do you think?"

Her gaze drifted downwards, meeting Shadow's tawny eyes that flickered up at her, like a silent confirmation. Beneath her hand, his coarse fur, a rough landscape of greys and blacks, slid and shifted, a comforting sensation as she stroked him.

"See, I knew you would agree with me," she sighed and continued looking through the website for what Mrs. Damascus had requested.

She'd spent the last two weeks in a flurry, tonight's party preparations still ringing in her ears while her mind raced through revised plans for the Damascus Turning Ball. Now, nervous energy propelled her as she hurried to dress, the silk of her bodycon dress whispering against her skin. She had to get to the party, the one she'd meticulously planned for Alena Deamonne, before the caterers arrived, but she had been racing against waiting for the sun to set.

She glanced once more in the mirror, her eyes catching the sleek silhouette of her tailored black dress clinging to her curves. The soft light illuminated the elegant lines. A loose bun framed her face, strands escaping to tickle her neck. The sweet scent of her red lip gloss filled the air as she touched it up, the cool smoothness of her hair between her fingers as she smoothed it before turning away.

The worn leather of her clutch nestled in her hand as she stepped out into the silvery, moonlit night. A cool breeze whispered against her skin as she walked to her car, the distant hum of crickets filling the air. The short drive ended at Taboos and Voodoos, a brick building devoid of windows. Two rusted steel doors loomed, the metallic scent mingling with the distinct, musky aroma of wolf shifters emanating from the two security guards. Magical ivy, thick and verdant, crawled along the left side of the building, tiny white flowers glowing softly in the night. The neon sign, flashing a pinkish red, pulsed with the club's name, casting an eerie glow on the already forming crowd. A kaleidoscope of scents filled the air as a menagerie of magickal creatures, vampires, witches, shifters, all buzzed with anticipation for the event to come.

The heavy oak door swung inward with a quiet whoosh, guided by the bouncer's hand. He offered a curt nod, his face illuminated by the neon glow spilling from within. No words were exchanged, but the scent of expensive cologne washed over her as she stepped inside. She was a familiar figure, her presence woven into the very fabric of the countless events she'd orchestrated within these walls. They recognized her, the silent acknowledgment a testament to her frequent presence, but she didn't recognize the bouncers.

Inside, the nightclub pulsed with a familiar energy. Round tables dotted the floor, their surfaces gleaming faintly in the dim light, while the dark wooden bar stretched along one wall. Behind it, shelves overflowed with an array of colorful potions and liquor bottles, catching the light. The stage bathed in a crimson glow, illuminating Shadow's Outcast as they hammered out a sound check, the sharp twang of guitar strings cutting through the air. Corbin, the wolf shifter, a solid figure with short dirty blonde hair and piercing yellow eyes, stood beside Allard, the vampire. Allard, a stark contrast with his long black hair, towered over him, his frame lean, eyes burning red. It wasn't her usual music, but the driving beat and raw vocals resonated surprisingly well.

Harlow spotted Desdemona Highmore near the bar, the owner of Magickal Morsels, her dark purple hair catching the light. She could almost smell the cinnamon and spices that always clung faintly to her clothes. Harlow started walking towards her, the low thrum of music vibrating through the floor. Before she could reach Desdemona, Alena materialized in her path. Harlow plastered on a smile, a wide curve of her lips that didn't touch the cool hazel of her eyes.

"Has the supply of blood from Onyx arrived?" Alena snorted, her foot tapping. "I just want to be prepared for anything bad before it happens. So please tell me all the mistakes that you have made now."

Harlow felt a shiver crawl up her spine, the scent of Alena's heavy perfume stinging her nostrils, as she strained to keep a pleasant smile plastered on her face. No matter how hard she tried, Alena always managed to grate on her nerves.

Alena's bleach-blonde hair seemed to glow under the bright lights, her blue eyes glinting with cool arrogance. The sharp tap-tap-tap of her red high heel against the polished floor could be heard slightly over the sound check. Towering over most women at almost six feet in those heels, she exuded a manufactured confidence. Her tan skin was a deep, unnatural orange shade, like a spray-painted sunset, and the skintight dress showcased her exaggerated curves like a sculpture. Harlow wondered with a silent sigh how much time and money Alena had spent to achieve such an unnaturally perfect image.

Taking a deep breath before she spoke, she looked Alena dead in the eyes. "I received the alert that Onyx already delivered exactly what you requested. I was just about to go verify everything was in order in the back. Please have a seat and order a drink. Everything is going according to plan and on schedule."

Walking around Alena, she continued her path towards Desdemona. "How are you doing today, Desi?"

"Oh, Harlow, there you are." Desdemona smiled, a sweet grin. She always looked so tiny, barely scraping four foot ten, and plump, radiating a cheery warmth like a freshly baked pie. Her purple hair, the color of ripe plums, was pulled back into a messy ponytail that bounced slightly as she moved. Her purple eyes, pools of shimmering amethyst, sparkled with an inner light, their warmth clear as she spoke. "I was just putting the finishing touches on the appetizers. The staff knows who to serve what types of food and drinks. I just spoke to Chilton, and he is in the kitchen in the back. I forgot how small the kitchen is here."

"Well, it is a club, not a restaurant," Harlow snickered.

"True," Desi huffed.

"Well, thank you again," Harlow sighed. "I don't know what I would have done if it hadn't been for your support. You have made moving here an easier transition."

"Anytime," Desi said, pulling her into a tight bear hug. "Well, I have left everything in capable hands and am going to go home and sleep. It has been a long day."

The scent of the witch's blood filled her nostrils as she stepped back, a surprisingly sweet aroma mingling with the tang, like the sugary treats Desi must have devoured, now staining the blood. "You go rest."

Looking over her shoulder, she watched Desi leave. Walking into the kitchen, the air thick with the scent of sweet and savory treats, was a bustle of servers and staff, their hurried footsteps a muted rhythm on the tile floor. Metal counters gleamed under the harsh fluorescent lights, filled with an array of platters with tasty baked delights.

Spotting Chilton directing staff, she walked towards him. Chilton's faux hawk, a striking black ombré to purple, stood tall and defiant. His hazel eyes, usually warm, were filled with a cool annoyance. He was tall and lanky, his shoulders hunched, as if weighed down, his hands jammed into his baggy jeans. A faded Shadow's Outcast tee, a relic from their last tour, stretched across his chest.

"Hey, Chilton," Harlow said.

The gravelly sound of his voice cut through the air, "Hey Harlow," he grunted, his brow furrowed into a deep V above his squinting eyes.

"Is everything alright?"

"Just the usual drama," he shrugged.

"Alright," she breathed, still not sure from his expression. "I just saw Desi, and from the look of it, she was accurate in that all the treats are here. Did Onyx deliver the blood?"

"Yeah," he nodded.

"Is there anything that did not arrive?"

"No. Everything on the checklist you sent me last week and again last night has arrived." Looking away from her, Chilton barked to a waiter, "Not there! Set that on the far table like I told you three times."

"Chilton," she exhaled. "What is wrong?"

"I just hate this part of these things," he smirked. "I am ready to be out there doing what I like and not here directing people around the kitchen."

"Would you like me to take over?"

"Yes," he smiled and then walked away without another word.

She shook her head, a silent rustle of hair against her cheek, and began speaking, her voice a low hum amidst the rising pre-opening cacophony. She gestured, a flurry of hands guiding the bustling staff as they prepared for the party. A glance at her watch revealed the doors would open in ten minutes. A heavy sigh escaped her lips. Against her own wishes, she went out, heading to check on Alena.

The low lights of the club cast long shadows as she walked across the floor. Up on the stage, she could see the band, instruments gleaming under the colored spotlights, ready to unleash a wave of sound. Alena near the bar was smoothing her dress out.

"You finally showed up again," Alena growled. "Remind me why I am paying you again?"

"Well, you're paying me to take care of the food, the decorations, the drinks," Harlow said in as steady a voice as she could. Her smile was sweet, and her eyes as innocent as she could make them as rage filled her. "I have made sure the blood is here and ready to use for cocktails. Also, the food is prepared and ready. The staff has been fully trained on what to feed what magickal. So if you had preferred, I could not have done those things and just stood around waiting for your next order instead."

Alena paused and looked at her. "Everything better go according to plan. The Damascus heir is supposed to be here tonight, and I need to make a good impression. If you ruin this night or ever talk to me like that, I will rip your throat out."

Harlow's heart stopped for a moment as a flash of forest green eyes ran through her memory. Exhaling her pent-up breath, she replied, "Everything is going to be exactly as you paid for."

Harlow

Chapter 5

Harlow's eyes darted around the club, catching the flashing strobes and blurry silhouettes of lingering patrons. She told herself it was to make sure everything was running smoothly, but a nervous flutter in her chest betrayed her real motive. The night seemed to go off without a hitch, the music fading into a low thrum, except Alena was still unhappy with everything she did. Standing behind Alena, with the cloying scent of spray tanner and over sprayed floral perfume prickling her nose, she waited, hoping to be dismissed. The party was technically over an hour ago, but Alena freaked out and would not let anyone leave as she waited for the star of the night.

"He hasn't shown up," Alena told one of her friends.

"Maybe something came up," the friend shrugged.

"Maybe it was that stray. He probably heard she was the coordinator for my party and didn't want to show up."

A prickling sensation crawled up Harlow's neck, raising gooseflesh in its wake, a physical manifestation of her rising temper. She inhaled deeply, the air catching in her throat, a silent battle waged against the red haze threatening to engulf her. No matter how hard she worked, this vamp would never be pleased.

"Isn't she planning his turning ball?" Her friend queried in a hesitant voice.

"That isn't the point," Alena snorted.

"Oh."

Alena's voice was a low growl. "I had on good word he would be here as an intro to our world," she hissed, her knuckles turning white as her hands clenched into tight fists. "I was supposed to introduce him to our world. Me! His own mother had set it up. There is only one reason he would not show up, and it's not me."

"You could always just show up at his place tomorrow to check up on him," her friend suggested tentatively.

"You're right, I could," Alena smirked. Harlow could almost hear the gears turning with whatever plan was clicking into place in Alena's head.

"I am sure he will fall under your alluring spell easily," her friend giggled as if she had gained confidence.

Laughing, Alena smoothed her hands down her body. "You're right."

She couldn't help the snort that escaped her lips as she turned it into a cough. *This woman is so obnoxiously narcissistic. Maybe she would be a good match for that male after all.* A wave of nausea, bitter and sharp, churned in her stomach as the thought bloomed. The image of Aris entwined with Alena felt like a punch to the gut, leaving her breathless and chilled.

"What do you want?" Alena sneered as she turned to glare at Harlow.

A flush crept up Harlow's neck, the warmth prickling her skin at being caught. She blinked as she fought to regain her composure.

"We have held the staff for an hour past the time of ending the party. We need to close things down now." Harlow tried to keep her voice sweet, but she could hear a hint of disdain tingeing her voice.

"Fine, whatever. This was a shitty party you threw, anyway." The words stung, sharp and cold, like a slap. Alena flicked her wrist, the movement a careless brush-off, dismissing everything with a flick. "I should have known better than to use After The Bite Events, especially since a stray runs it."

Harlow's fists clenched, a burning anger rising to defend her work. She wanted to insist she'd delivered exactly what was asked, her throat tight with fury. But the cold, indifferent faces, years of being an outsider screamed and taught her she would never be heard. With a defeated sigh, she pivoted sharply, the click of her heels sharp against the polished floor and sought the dim solace of the bar.

Chilton stood there leaning on the polished mahogany bar. His low voice, a gravelly murmur, mingled with the clinking of glasses as he gabbed with a guest, their laughter a brief counterpoint to the low hum of the tavern.

"Turn the lights on and tell everyone it's cleanup time." She looked over her shoulder, hoping the cleanup would not take too long as she had to be home by 5:00 a.m., before sunrise, and it was already 3:00 a.m.

Chilton sighed and began the familiar closing process. The staff, a well-oiled machine, moved with practiced efficiency, the clatter of chairs and spray of cleaning fluid filling the air. By 4:30 a.m., the harsh fluorescent lights still buzzing overhead, she slipped out before the final mop strokes, the faint scent of disinfectant clinging to her clothes. A pang of guilt tightened her chest as she started the drive home.

A sigh escaped her lips as she shrugged out of the dress, the silken fabric whispering as it slid to the floor in a shimmering pool. Shadow, a silent hunter, padded around the room, his paws making no sound on the floor. She reached for her most comforting dressing gown, a floor-length eyelet cotton nightgown with tiny, embroidered flowers, each a splash of pastel color. The cool, soft cotton felt like a gentle caress against her skin as she padded back into the living room. She reached for her book, its pages slightly rough under her fingertips, but a sharp knock echoed through the quiet apartment, making her pause. Her heart hammered against her ribs as she walked to the door, the sound of her bare feet muffled by the rug. She glanced at the clock, its gentle tick a counterpoint to her racing pulse, and knew the first pale light of dawn would just be painting the sky outside.

Inhaling deeply, she caught a whiff of human blood. Her breath hitched, her heart seemed to stop while she cautiously opened the door. Every thought left her brain as she tried to register what was going on. Her mouth opened and then closed before it opened again, saying one of the many thoughts circling like a buzzard in her head. "Are you stalking me?"

He smiled as he pushed the door open a bit more. "Who said I'm stalking you? I'm just good at research."

Her skin prickled with heat as his gaze, a tangible warmth, drifted down her body. A flush bloomed across her chest, and she instinctively wanted to disappear, the whisper-thin fabric suddenly betraying her. But she was defenseless, with only her own trembling hands available to offer a meager shield as she crossed them over her chest.

She tilted her chin up, the movement crisp and defiant against the imagined weight of his gaze, and

spoke, her voice even despite the tremor she felt inside. "How did you find out where I live?"

He winked, a playful glint in his eye as he leaned against the doorjamb, the door creaked slightly under his weight.

"Could you please answer my question?" she said harshly. She unfolded her arms and then pressed her palms flat against her thighs. This devastatingly gorgeous human was twenty-one years old, she reminded herself, a silent mantra against the rush of blood in her ears. Even if she were perpetually trapped in her nineteen-year-old body, she would ensure her reaction didn't betray her true age.

"I called in a favor or two," he murmured. His hand shot up and gently brushed her hair off her cheek.

Startled, she jumped at the fire of his touch. "I need to go inside before the sun comes out fully," she murmured, her cheeks blazing.

"I just wanted to check in and see if you..." he seemed to pause dramatically. "Needed anything. Questions or..."

The unfinished question hung heavy in the still air with unspoken words, as her eyes grew wide, mirroring her shock. Before she could formulate a response, his hand, warm and firm, cradled the back of her neck, pulling her in.

"Do your lips taste as good as they look?" he murmured just a breath away.

His warm breath, carrying a hint of mint, fluttered across her face like a gentle breeze before his lips, soft and inviting, pressed against hers. Her own parted without conscious thought. A rush of heat flooded her senses as his tongue, a velvet touch, swept into her mouth, a sweet, spicy taste of cinnamon exploding on her palate. The faint sound of his heartbeat drummed in her ears as his hands pulled her closer, the rough denim of his jacket a stark contrast to the sudden tenderness of his touch. She felt herself melt into his strong embrace, her muscles relaxing, her body molding to his. All coherent thoughts scattered like brightly colored leaves caught in a sudden, fierce gust of wind, leaving only the feeling of him.

A soft, insistent mewing, a delicate thread in the thick, fog-like haze of lust, pressed into her; he stirred within her a warmth she had not experienced before. She ignored the sound; her skin flushed. But the mewing grew louder, a plaintive cry cutting through the heavy air, until she could no longer deny its presence. With a frustrated huff, she shoved him away. The soft breeze hit her heated skin, her hand coming up to gingerly touch her swollen lips.

His face lit up with a wide smile as he reached for her again. She swatted his hand away, the light smack echoing in the otherwise quiet room, while his laughter, warm and husky, filled the air. She pushed him again, the soft thud of contact a prelude to her next move. With a sharp creak, she grabbed the door and slammed it shut, the resounding bang vibrating through the frame. Leaning against the cool, smooth wood, she slid down. She knew she was in for a world of trouble if she didn't make sure that male understood she could not be with him. Even if it's just for a night. *He is human; I should have never let him kiss me. They will kill me if I even remotely think of biting the prodigal son.* She squeezed her eyes shut, and a shiver traced its way down her spine. She wondered, a knot forming in her stomach, if the local vampire coven would descend upon her as soon as the darkness fell.

Johnna Dee

After the Bite Events

Aris

Chapter 6

Aris stood outside her door, a smirk playing on his lips, the rising sun sending rays of light glinting across the lawn. The faint sounds of music and city noise drifted over from the street. He didn't know why but getting under her skin felt like a guilty pleasure. Tonight, he should have made a cameo at Alena's party. Instead, he'd abandoned his guards, the heavy weight of responsibility replaced by a light thrill. It hadn't taken long to find Harlow. She didn't have an actual office, so she had her home listed on her business licenses.

He'd planned a simple conversation but tasting her had become an irresistible impulse. Bathed in the soft glow of the lamp behind her, the silhouette of her curves beneath the nightgown had been a siren's call. Her lips, a warm invitation he couldn't refuse. Now, the phantom sweetness lingered on his tongue. He itched to pound on the door until she opened up, and taste her again, but the memory of those wide, hazel eyes, the firm pressure of her hands pushing him away, warned him against it.

He turned and walked to the road. The streetlights cast a hazy yellow glow on the asphalt. Soon, he spotted the sleek black limo, its chrome glinting under the artificial light, crawling along the road, undoubtedly searching for him. He knew his actions would annoy his mother. He could almost hear her sharp tone already, for his failure to attend the party. But the very idea of making small talk with the self-absorbed, whose perfume was as fake as her smile, trying too hard to look human like, Alena, was the last thing he wanted. The thought alone made his skin crawl. He didn't understand why his mother kept trying to push them together, other than her family's high rank within the coven. But status didn't equate to substance. She was simply, undeniably, uninteresting.

Climbing into the car, the driver looked at him with worried eyes. "Just drive me home," he murmured. "No need to tell my mom you lost me."

The chauffeur offered nothing, but a deflated sigh, the sound like air hissing from a punctured tire, before pressing the accelerator. The engine rumbled to life, a low growl that vibrated faintly through the car.

He fished his phone from his pocket and opened PixelTome, plunging into doom scrolling. The bright screen blurred as his thumb swiped, image after image flashing by, none holding his attention. His mind wandered, replaying the memory of her. The heat of his own skin contrasted with the cool silkiness of hers. He remembered the fire of her body against his, a blaze he knew she'd deny feeling. But he had seen it—a fleeting spark in her eyes, a subtle shift in her posture. It was there; he was sure of it, as strong for her as the magnetic pull he felt. Or at least, he hoped it was.

The tires crunched, a gritty song underneath him, as they turned off the smooth asphalt and onto the driveway. The garage door clicked open, the sound echoing in the otherwise still garage. He slipped into the cool dimness of the kitchen. A murmur of distant voices drifted from the living room, soft and indistinct, like the hum of bees. Frowning, a knot of unease tightening in his stomach, he crept towards the stairs, hoping to ascend unnoticed before his mother's sharp ears picked up his presence. He couldn't decipher the unfamiliar voice, and the mystery made him retreat, since her visitors were a rare daytime occurrence, since they wouldn't be able to leave.

"There he is," Amara said in a scolding tone. "We have a guest who came to check on you since you didn't make it to the party. I explained that you were not feeling well."

Aris paused halfway up the creaking stairs. He turned and looked down at his mom and Alena. A knot twisted in his stomach as he realized, with a sickening lurch, that his mom already knew he hadn't gone to the party. He could see her clearly in the soft, warm light of the foyer. Her arms were akimbo, a silent challenge, while one perfectly arched brow rose, a clear expression of disapproval etched upon her face.

Coughing, he replied, "Yes, I am feeling under the weather. I am just going to bed now. Don't want to get anyone sick. Goodnight."

"Oh, no," Alena sighed dramatically.

Aris spun around, the steps creaking softly under his shoes, but stopped short. His mother's voice, sharp and cold as a winter wind, cut through him.

"Not so fast, young man."

He pivoted, his gaze locking onto his mother. A slow, wicked smile crept across her face, the subtle curve catching the light, and he heard the faintest, almost silent sound of her pleased sigh. He felt a chill run down his spine, sensing the beginning of something mischievous in the air.

Amara's voice was now sickeningly sweet. "Our guest has offered to nurse you back to health. With the understanding that if she bites you, she'll not make it to sunrise."

Aris glared at his mother, knowing full well she was torturing him. "Mom, it's been a long... hmm... a very long time since you were human, so maybe I

should explain it to you. The best cure for being sick is sleep. So, I am just going to go up to my room and do just that."

"Oh, no, I have been raising you your whole life." Amara shook her head, a cascade of blonde hair shimmering in the light. "I know the best cure is soup. Alena has told me what a superb cook she is of human food. So, she is going to make you a nice bowl of soup. Walk yourself to the kitchen *now*."

The way she said now had Aris frowning. "I highly doubt Ms. Deamonne has ever seen the inside of a kitchen, let alone the inside of a fridge."

"I have seen plenty of kitchens and know exactly what to make for you," Alena demurred, batting her eyelashes. "Just show me the way. Plus, there is no need to be formal; just call me Alena."

"Yes, Aris, show her the way." Amara's glare pierced him, making him feel like a scolded boy once more. The air crackled with unspoken reprimands, a silent echo of past misdeeds. He remembered that exact look; the afternoon sun warm on his back as he scaled the rough bark of the old oak, followed by the stinging scrape on his knee when he fell. After the cool salve and gentle touch on his wound, she had pinned him with this same gaze, patiently explaining the vital importance of not bleeding in a house full of vampires.

Rolling his eyes, he jogged down the stairs and led the way to the kitchen. With a sweep of his arm, he showed off the kitchen. "Here you go, the kitchen."

"Oh, I will make you a perfect soup," Alena said, walking over to him.

Alena reached out, her fingers brushing against the rough fabric of his shirt as she placed her hand on his chest. A furrow appeared on his brow, a silent

crease forming as he gently peeled her hand away. "Let's see about this soup." Out of the corner of his eye, he saw his mother start to leave. "Mother dearest, don't we need a chaperone?"

Whirling around, Amara started. "What?"

"I know how old-fashioned you are," Aris smirked knowingly. "So, again, don't we need a chaperone so nothing *untoward* happens?"

He could see the muscle twitching in Amara's cheek. Finally, she spoke, "Yes." A forced smile spread across her face.

He sauntered over, the wooden stool scraping against the floor as he settled onto it. Amara mirrored him, a frustrated huff escaping her lips. The palpable heat of his mother's anger radiated off her in shimmering waves, yet her gaze remained fixed, distant, and unreadable.

Alena wandered the kitchen, the scent of old spices hanging in the air. Cupboard doors creaked open and slammed shut, a staccato rhythm accompanying her frantic search. Canned goods clattered onto the counter, their labels a bright jumble against the surface. Sugar granules spilled, catching the light like tiny diamonds. A coarse shake of salt, a puff of sharp pepper—the motley collection of ingredients hinted at the culinary disaster to come, solidifying the feeling that her attempt at soup would be anything but appetizing.

Alena's voice, a relentless hum, filled the air as she rambled about the latest purse she had snared at Hexquisite Hems. He tried to retreat into the glowing world of PixelTome, but each time he dared to lift it, his mother's hand would descend, pushing the device back down with a decisive thud. *Apparently, Mom's decided if she's going to listen to this vapid rambling, I will have to as well.* The buzz of Alena's voice droned on, listing celebrities that had the same purse. He laid his head on the cool, smooth countertop, the scent of lemon cleaner stinging his nostrils. Suddenly, his mother's sharp grip seized his hair, a painful yank forcing his head up with a grunt.

Looking at his mom, he mouthed, "Why do you hate me?"

Her eyes widened, a flicker of surprise in their depths, before she sprang to her feet. She crossed to a nearby drawer and pulled it open with a quiet thud. From within, she retrieved a slim notebook and a pen that clicked softly as she uncapped it. He watched her and arched a questioning eyebrow, the gesture silent but full of curiosity.

Scribbling on the pad, she wrote, *I don't hate you.*

Grabbing the pen, he scrolled ink across the page. *Then why do you constantly try to get me to hang out with the vapid princess?*

Her eyes scanned the words printed on the paper before a frustrated sigh escaped her lips. With a swift grab, she crushed the paper into a tight ball, the sound a soft crackle. She then shoved the crumpled paper into her pocket, her expression unreadable.

Alena's voice, a relentless drone, spewed the coven's latest gossip. He leaned back, the wood of the chair back digging into his back and stared at the ornate ceiling. Arms crossed tight, he braced, expecting his mom's inevitable lecture. But a thick, heavy silence, punctuated only by Alena's voice, hung in the air.

"It's done!" Alena exclaimed.

He lowered his head, eyes sweeping over the chaotic landscape of the counters. Sticky spills formed

shimmering pools under the dim kitchen light. The air hung thick with a sickeningly sweet, yet sharp peppery scent that stung his nostrils. His stomach churned, a wave of nausea rising with the cloying odor. She placed the bowl down, the messy soup sloshing over its rim—a thick, lumpy brown mess that defied description, its ingredients an unidentifiable mystery.

"Here," Alena said, shoving a spoon into his chest.

He held the spoon, his eyes darting to his mother. She nodded expectantly. He knew that was a twisted form of punishment, but he was too old to be punished. He dipped the spoon in. Swirling it, expected it to melt like it was a vat of acid, but the spoon still held its shape. He glanced at his mother again, hoping for a reprieve. The stench filled his nostrils again, almost burning the hairs in his nose. Dipping the spoon in, he scooped up a small bit and brought it to his lips. He gagged, swallowing it.

"Isn't it yummy?" Alena smiled.

His eyes darted to his mother, who nodded slightly. "Mmm," he murmured, unable to come up with a suitable lie.

"I knew you would love it," Alena rambled. "I have seen the cook do this before for the servants. It didn't look that hard at all."

Heaving himself up, he stumbled towards the stainless steel refrigerator. He plucked out a soda can, its condensation slick against his clammy palm, desperate to eradicate the lingering, vomit-inducing taste clinging to his tongue. A wave of nausea rolled over him, a souvenir from the swill Alena dared call soup. He tipped his head back; the fizz tickling his nose as he gulped down the entire can, the sugary sweetness a sharp contrast to the lingering foulness. At least the taste was gone, replaced by the tang of the soda.

"I would make a wonderful wife, don't you think, Aris?" Alena said, coming up behind him. Her hand rubbed his back.

He couldn't control the coughing spasm that hit him while he tried to find words.

Johnna Dee

Harlow

Chapter 7

Harlow had slept fitfully all day, the silence amplifying her anxiety. She waited for her phone to ping with a message that felt like a death knell, but the screen remained dark. Now, the cool leather of her car seat pressed against her back as she sat parked before the imposing Damascus manor house. The looming stone facade seemed to whisper threats in the gentle breeze. She gripped the steering wheel; her knuckles white, struggling to summon the courage to step out into the twilight air.

"Harlow," she grumbled to herself. "Don't be a big baby! *Go* inside and face the music."

With a soft rush of air, she exhaled, squeezing her eyes shut. Her hand, trembling slightly, found the cool metal of the door handle. She shoved the heavy door open, its hinges creaking. Her whole body was stiff, each muscle screaming in protest as she walked towards the entrance. The brass bell echoed with a hollow ding-dong that seemed to reverberate in the pit of her stomach as dread washed over her. Looking down, she smoothed the crisp navy-blue fabric of her skirt.

The same human butler opened the heavy oak door. He guided her through the dimly lit hallway, the scent of beeswax and lemon cleaner, to the same drawing-room as before. Aris's face, illuminated by the warm glow of the fireplace, broke into a welcoming smile as he crossed the plush rug towards her. His hand, surprisingly warm against the chill of her silk blouse, gently gripped her elbow, guiding her towards the couch.

"It's so nice to see you again, Harlow," Aris murmured, winking conspiratorially.

"Ms. Rathmore," Amara snorted.

"Yes?" Harlow frowned, the disdain in Amara's voice hitting her like a splash of cold water. She felt the tightening in her brow as it furrowed, a visible sign of her inner turmoil. She worried her lip, the soft skin now slightly raw under her fang.

"Oh my," Amara smiled sweetly. "I wasn't talking to you. It's the boy. I keep trying to teach him manners, but he persists in being... oh... what's the word... frustrating. So please forgive his lack of manners, Ms. Rathmore."

"No, no, no," Harlow shook her head. The fear that had been clawing at her started to dissipate when she realized they might not know what happened. "You do not need to apologize for..." she waved her hand around. "Anything. Please, you can call me Harlow. Well, to get down to business, I—"

"Let's have a drink before business," Aris interrupted. Her eyes flicked to the side, catching the curve of his lips pulled into a cocky smirk.

Amara huffed out a breath of air. "Fine, pour everyone a drink."

Harlow froze, the words catching in her throat. The scene she'd constructed in her mind dissolved, replaced by the muted reality before her.

The rhythmic slosh of liquid meeting glass echoed in the dimly lit room. A cloying aroma of fruity sweetness mingled with warm spices and earthy richness hung heavy in the air as he poured whiskey into a

crystal tumbler. Next, he filled two glasses with viscous, crimson juice, the metallic tang sharp in contrast to the sweet nectar that made her mouth water. She tasted anticipation, realizing she had forgotten to drink before her nervous departure. He offered the first blood-filled glass to his mother, who accepted it demurely, the red liquid staining her lips as she took a delicate sip.

He circled the dark, polished coffee table, the wood gleaming faintly in the lamplight. He extended the glass to her; the crimson swirled. His fingers, warm and slightly rough, lingered a moment too long, a feather-light brush against the delicate skin of her hand, sending a shiver up her arm. His knowing smile spread across his face as he spoke, "I hope you enjoy this one; it comes from a local witch who eats quite healthy. She is a vegan and—."

"Aris," Amara growled. "Please sit down; she doesn't care about our locally sourced blood. I am going to batty-fang your hide later if you don't quit acting out. We can get down to business now."

Amara and Aris exchanged a silent glance. Amara's brow furrowed, her lips a thin line—annoyance radiating like a visible heat haze. Aris, in contrast, wore a smirk, a silent chuckle dancing in his eyes as if he were enjoying the silent, unseen battle crackling in the air between them.

"Now that we have had a drink," Aris said as he tossed back the whole glass of whiskey in one swallow. "We can now get back to business. And to speak in the dialect of the current era, so quit giving me mouth-pie, Mom."

Amara's lips parted, a silent 'O' forming before snapping shut. She tried again, the corners of her mouth twitching, then a bright, tinkling laugh finally erupted, filling the air like wind chimes. "My sweet little lambkin." She shook her head as she patted the space next to her. Turning to Harlow, a warm smile spread across Amara's face. "Please show us the revisions that have been made."

Aris sat next to Amara. Those green eyes seemed to look into the darkest depths of her soul as they never left hers.

Her throat bobbed with a nervous gulp, then she slid the plans across the table. Her gaze fixed on the intricate lines, avoiding Aris's piercing stare. Harlow's pen scratched softly on the paper as she diligently noted the changes Amara requested.

A dry, rasping sound of a throat clearing sliced through the room, making heads turn toward the butler in the doorway. His face a mask of professional expectation as he stared at Amara as if waiting for a cue. Amara gave a decisive nod. With a soft rustle of her silk gown, she stood up.

"Please excuse me," Amara said, darting a fleeting angry glare at Aris. "I will be back in a few. I have coven business to attend to."

Aris trailed behind his mother to the door. A soft click echoed in the sudden quiet as he shut it. "Don't worry, she'll be a moment. She must end some poor vamp's delusions."

"Umm," Harlow said. "Alright."

"We didn't get to finish our conversation earlier," he whispered as he sat down next to her.

"What conversation?" Harlow laughed. She brimmed with questions, a tempest of inquiries swirling in her mind, yet she steeled her gaze, masking her eagerness behind a wall of practiced indifference. "We were not discussing anything."

"Now that you mention it," he said, tapping his finger on his chin. "You're right; we weren't talking."

His hand flashed out, the sudden movement a blur as he seized the back of her neck. She gasped, a strangled sound lost in the suddenness of his touch, and her hands flew up, palms flat against his chest, trying to shove him away. But his grip was like iron, unyielding, and her own strength felt like water. Then his mouth slammed down on hers, a brutal, possessive claim. Her fingers, balled into fists, dug into the fabric of his shirt, a fleeting impulse to hurt him flickering through her. But then his tongue was there, a warm invasion, and the fight drained out of her, leaving her weak and trembling. The sharp, smoky tang of whiskey filled her mouth, mingling with the taste of him, stealing her breath and her will.

His hand, a silent predator, crept up her skirt, the calloused palm a stark contrast to the soft skin of her thighs. A shiver ran down her spine as he slid between her thighs. For a split second, a protest flickered in her mind, but the delicate caress, feather-light and insistent, painted fire across her skin, diving deeper. The whisper of silk as his warm fingers pushed her panties aside, the intoxicating dance as they circled her nub, stole her breath. A gasp escaped her lips as her hips bucked in involuntary response. Then, the world exploded as one warm finger slid inside, a deep, carnal invasion, while his thumb continued its maddening circle. One hand, trembling, reached down, her fingers clenching around his wrist. Her mind screamed to pull that hand out, to reclaim control, but her traitorous hand wouldn't listen, wouldn't obey.

The desire to taste him was a tidal wave, crashing over her senses. She bit her lip, a futile attempt to stem the need, tasting the metallic tang of her own blood as her fangs pierced the soft flesh. A salty, bitter warmth flooded her mouth. Another finger, slick and insistent, slid inside, mimicking the rhythm building within. A wild storm, a vortex of raw sensation, brewed in her core, stirred into being by his touch. She could feel the electric anticipation crackling through her.

"Gods, you're so wet," he murmured next to her ear. His lips closed around her earlobe, the wet suction a warm contrast to the cool air. Her fingers dug into his wrist, nails grazing his skin as his hand moved rhythmically, a slick, insistent pressure against her flesh.

Releasing her lobe, he muttered, "Fuck. Mom's coming back."

He pulled his hand away, the air cool against her damp core, and smoothed the silk of her skirt, the fabric whispering under his touch. He then brought his fingers to his mouth, his eyes never leaving hers, and she watched, breathless, as he slowly licked the remnants of her juice. A jolt, a sudden, sharp clench in her core, shattered the moment as the click of the door echoed in the sudden silence.

Amara looked around the room, then said, "Did my lambkin say some grievous thing?"

Aris pulled his fingers out of his mouth and smirked.

"What?" Harlow asked, her brow furrowed.

"You look like you've seen a ghost, and he looks a little too smug," Amara stated, tapping her foot. "What did the boy do?"

Harlow whispered, "Oh, no." She shook her head, a desperate attempt to dislodge the emotions that buzzed like angry hornets through her veins. The frantic movement did nothing to ease the tightening pressure in her core. "He said nothing. Is there anything else you want to add? For the party, that is."

Amara's eyes seemed to search Harlow's face, lingering on every contour, and every flicker of emotion. She inhaled sharply, the air catching in her throat as she tried her best to compose herself, her hands trembling slightly at her sides.

"No," Amara smiled a cool, disdainful smile. "Please let me know when you have the revisions done."

"I will." She gathered the leather portfolio, its smooth surface cool against her fingertips. She walked towards the front door, the soft click of her heels echoing on the polished floor. Her hand, now resting on the cold metal of the doorknob, paused as his voice, a low rumble, stopped her.

"Big plans this weekend?" Aris whispered from behind her.

The frantic pounding of her heart had been so loud, so all-consuming, as she focused solely on escaping, she hadn't heard his advance, nor caught the faint scent of his cologne drifting in the air.

"Yes," she replied.

"Anything fun?"

"Yes, I am scheduled to have so much fun."

His voice deepened as he spoke. "Is your definition of a fun weekend in bed with me?"

A flush crept up her neck, blooming into a fierce heat on her cheeks that she could feel radiating outwards.

"Aris," Amara scolded. "Go to your father's office and deal with the mess you created."

He huffed, the sound echoing slightly in the oth-

erwise silent room, and with a dramatic roll of his eyes, the whites flashing briefly in the dim light; he turned and left; the door clicked shut behind him with a dull thud.

Amara walked over to her. "I have tried to tell the boy to leave you be, but obviously that isn't working. So, I am going to tell you. He is young and wants to go after a pretty little thing, but he will grow bored soon. For your own best interest, nip it in the bud now."

"I understand." Harlow nodded, looking down at her feet.

Amara's fingers grasped her chin, lifting her face. "Make sure you tell him you are not interested." Amara's voice, a low hum, vibrated in the air. Harlow's eyes, wide and uncertain, met Amara's narrowed gaze, slits that seemed to dissect Harlow's very being.

"I've tried," Harlow whispered, feeling the weight of that glare pressing down on her.

"Then say it louder next time." The sharpness of her words hung in the air like a lingering scent of burnt sugar. Amara spun on her heel as she walked away, the click of her heels fading as she walked away, her stiff back a silent testament to her displeasure.

Johnna Dee

After the Bite Events

Aris

Chapter 8

In the dimly lit office, the scent of old books and leather hung heavy in the air. Aris rolled his shoulders, the cotton of his shirt feeling rough against his skin. The tap of a pen punctuated the quiet of the room. Until this morning, his mother harbored some delusional idea of him marrying Alena and forging a deeper bond within the Coven. But apparently, after sitting and listening to Alena talk, her voice a monotonous drone of vapidness, she decided that was a bad idea.

"Your mom means well," Tiberias laughed. "I have explained to the Deamonne's that you are otherwise preoccupied."

The gruffness in his dad's voice was a low rumble that caused each hair on his arms to prickle with unease. "Occupied how?" he snapped.

"My bit-o-jam means well, boy," Tiberias sighed.

"What exactly does that mean?" Aris growled.

"We have tried to keep you from the politics aspect of our community, but now that you are about to be turned, it's time you step up to your position in our coven. That position comes with certain... expectations."

"So, what is it exactly that you guys are expecting me to do that's considered *stepping* up?" A shiver crawled up Aris's spine, an icy whisper against his skin, as the question hung in the air. Every fiber in his being screamed a warning, a cacophony of dread, telling him he would not, could not, like the answer.

"Creating alliances," Tiberias whispered, flushing as his eyes would not meet Aris'.

"How would I create *alliances?*" The red flush crept up his neck as he glared at his father. A low growl rumbled in his chest, mirroring the thunder he could almost taste on his tongue. His fists clenched, the nails digging crescents into his palms, as the bitter scent of resentment filled his nostrils.

"We are going to introduce you to the daughters of a few local covens, which might lead to an alliance," Tiberias sighed, leaning back in his chair as he stared up at the ceiling.

"I assume you guys have already decided who I am supposed to spend the rest of eternity with," Aris said, his voice deceptively low.

"No," Tiberias grumbled. "We just have some women for you to meet."

"That's a hard pass." Aris shook his head. "I can handle my love life without your interference."

"Just meet them and—"

"No!" Aris slammed his fist on his father's desk. "You either don't interfere in my love life, or I leave and never come back. Make your choice."

Tiberias sighed, the sound like a deflated bellows. He rested his face in his hands. "You know what we'll choose."

"Say it like you mean it then," Aris grunted. A crimson haze clouded his vision as he tried to quell the furious fire that blazed in his veins. He could almost hear the frantic thumping of his heart in his ears, a re-

lentless drumbeat fueling the inferno. The metallic tang of adrenaline stung his tongue as he fought to regain control, each ragged breath a scorching wave against the rising tide of rage.

"We will stay out of your love life, but," Tiberias paused as if debating his next words. "*We* are going to introduce you to people at required social events; just keep an open mind. You would never be forced by us to be with any of them."

"Again," Aris shrugged. He clenched and un-clenched his fists. "I don't need or want help in that arena. I'll be nice to whoever you introduce me to, diplomatic if you will, but nothing more will happen."

"Boy, you're young and you'll—"

"I'm tired of hearing how young I am. If I am sooooo young, then maybe you should put off for a few more years turning me. Maybe once I'm," he made air quotes, "old enough you can turn me."

Tiberias seemed to mull over Aris's words; his brow furrowed in concentration. Aris's thoughts, mean-while, were running in frantic circles, a hamster on a squeaky, never-ending wheel, each rotation bringing him no closer to an answer, a dizzying and frustrating sensation.

Tiberias frowned. "I'm sorry. You're right. You are older than I was when I made the choice, so you are old enough to decide your own love life. Shit, you're older than I was when I met and married Ama-ra."

"While we're rehashing history," Aris started and then stopped.

"Do we have to?" Tiberias laughed. "This con-versation has already gotten out of control."

"Your control," Aris snorted. "But I want to know where I came from."

Tiberias's brow furrowed as he ran a hand through his dirty blonde hair. "You don't."

"Are you going to tell me I'm too young to know what I want to know now?"

"No, let me rephrase it. I don't. There are some things better left alone."

"In that case," Aris said, standing up. He walked out, slamming the door with a loud thud.

He saw her jump; the blood draining from her already pale face in the dim light that spilled from the room. She had been pressing against the door, and getting caught eavesdropping made her steps falter.

"My lambkin, I want—" Amara started.

"Not interested." Aris's voice was a low growl, laced with annoyance as he bounded up the stairs, his boots thudding on the steps. Reaching his room, he threw the door open with a sharp bang that echoed through the silent house, then the distinct click of the lock reverberated, sealing him away in his sanctuary.

He slammed the door to his room, before locking it.

A small knock, before a tentative voice spoke, "Aris, please."

"Nope." Grabbing his phone, he connected to the Bluetooth speaker system and started blaring music. *If they don't want to talk about the things I want to talk about, then we can just not talk for now.*

Damascus Coven

The moment the sun painted the sky with strokes of warm gold, he crept outside. The metallic red of his car gleamed in the morning light as he slid inside and sped away. With the press of a button, the top lowered, and the cool morning breeze, carrying the scent of damp earth and blooming honeysuckle, rushed through his dirty blonde hair, whipping strands across his face. The sun warmed his skin. A ribbon of asphalt against the green hills, the winding curves of the road ahead momentarily distracted him from the storm of thoughts raging in his mind. The engine hummed at a steady rhythm.

Anger swirled in him mixed with sadness, while he slowed down and entered town. He had no destination in mind; he just needed out. All his life he had asked where he came from. He got no answers. When he was eighteen, he had hired a local detective to do research on his birth, but there were no answers. No official adoption records, no records showing he came from another country—it was like he just appeared one day at one month old. *It seems the closer I get to turning the more I want to know about my past. Every avenue I took to explore it was another dead end. Then throw in the stress of having to live up to standards I am not sure I can meet. They are throwing vamp tramps my way like I am some prize at a carnival game to send off to the best pitcher.*

The vibrant sign, a beacon of color, snagged his attention, compelling him to steer into an empty parking space. Through the expansive plate windows, a dazzling array of merchandise winked, catching the light. He crossed the threshold, the scent of new leather and polished wood filling his nostrils, and wandered aimlessly, his footsteps echoing softly on the polished floor, unsure of his quarry. Then, amidst the gleaming displays, it materialized, a siren call to his senses, and he knew. *She probably will not like it.* The insidious whisper of self-doubt slithered into his ear. He shrugged it off, the weight of it momentarily settling on his shoulders like a leaden cloak. Picking up the item, he headed towards the checkout.

He drove the last couple of blocks, arriving at the apartment complex. The sun, a white-hot glare in the sky, beat down on his shoulders, almost blinding him. He walked through the courtyard, the scent of freshly cut grass heavy in the air and climbed the concrete stairs to her floor. He noted her door was shrouded in shadow, a cool darkness promising she'd open it without fear. His tongue traced his lips, remembering the ghost of her sweet taste. He knocked, the sound echoing in the still air, but no response came. *She's probably asleep.* He debated, leaving or if he should try again? He knocked louder this time; the sound echoed and heard a muffled shout from within. The heavy wooden door cracked open with a groan, revealing hazel eyes peering out from a crack. Shock colored those eyes, widening them.

"Are you trying to get me killed? The sun is out." She closed the door with a soft thud. He shoved his boot in the small crack before she could shut him out.

"I noticed that when the sun is out your door is in shade," he smirked. "I know you picked a place where you can avoid the sun as much as possible. Here." He handed her the bag, shoving it in the gap.

"What's this?" she asked, trying to push the shopping bag back out.

He pushed his hand against the door, shoving it

open ever so slightly. "Take the gift."

"Fine," she murmured, grabbing the bag handle.

His hand lingered on her fingers before he relinquished the Hexquisite Hems shopping bag.

Her eyes looked wary as she opened the bag. She looked inside, her eyes growing big. "This is too much, I can't—"

"It's nothing," he shrugged.

"To a rich boy like you, it's nothing," she grumbled.

"We both know I am not a boy, so never call me that again."

"No, you are. I am a century older than you. So, you are a boy. Spending your parents' money doesn't make you grown up." She shoved the bag against his chest.

"Why are you fighting this?" he murmured, reaching in to stroke her cheek.

"I... I... I'm not—" she stuttered.

"Lying to yourself?" he laughed sardonically. "Stop fighting this. We both know you want it as much as I do."

"No," she said with a shaky voice.

Pushing the door open. He stepped in. "You can deny to others, but I know you feel the same pull I do."

She shook her head, her dark hair swaying like a silken curtain. "I am not interested," she said, the words flat, yet her voice, though meant to sound firm, held a wavering, almost pleading quality that betrayed her

lack of conviction.

He filled his lungs, the delicate floral notes of her perfume swirling around him. His gaze, unwavering, locked onto her as he moved forward, the door left ajar. She halted when her back pressed against the wall. His eyes traced her form, lingering on the crisp white cotton of her dress that softly caressed her lithe curves. The leather tips of his boots nudged against the delicate tips of her toes.

"I can prove you wrong," he whispered, his mouth a breath away.

"Please," she whispered.

The dim light of the room made it hard to read her expression. Was that a plea to stop etched on her face, or was it a silent urging to continue? Her voice was soft, lost somewhere between a whimper and a sigh, leaving him unsure.

He dropped to his knees, her skin smooth beneath his touch as he touched her ankles, sliding the dress upwards. Her eyes, pools of dark chocolate, flickered with a mix of pleading and fiery anticipation. As his hands reached her hips, he encountered the soft barrier of her white cotton panties. A harsh rip echoed in the silent room as the fabric tore and fell to the floor. His hands now firm on her hips, dug slightly into the delicate flesh. His breath, warm and ragged, fluttered across her softness. A soft moan, like the rustle of silk, escaped her lips, her hands gripping his hair tightly. He flicked his tongue across her clit; the action sending a shiver through her as her muscles tensed beneath his touch. Feeling bolder, he sucked her clit into his mouth, the wet sound filling the space as his hand slipped around, and two digits sliding inside her. She clenched around his fingers, a hot, tight grip as he thrust them in and out of her. Her hands pulled at his hair, urging him closer, pushing his head closer to her.

He tasted the musky sweetness, the intoxicating nectar of her desire. Soon, her legs began to tremble, a visible tremor that ran through her entire body, as her hands moved to his shoulders, digging into the skin.

His arm encircled her, a sturdy anchor as her legs buckled, the sudden weakness sending a pleasant shiver through him. His mouth continued its insistent exploration, a warm, wet pressure against her skin, while his hand boldly traced the curve of her hip. He lifted one leg, the soft skin of her calf sliding against his shoulder as he cupped her ass, his fingers molding to her shape.

He flicked his tongue across her bundle of nerves one last time before she growled, "Aris!"

He loosened his grip, letting her slide down the wall. His eyes locked with hers, catching the glint in their depths. He saw it—the satiation and the crimson bloom of bloodlust—like a wildfire in her gaze. The air hung thick with the metallic tang of fresh blood. He knew that look and had witnessed its chilling beauty enough to recognize the silent roar, the unspoken hunger. It was time to retreat, to put distance between them before that hunger turned his way.

Standing up, he walked out the open door. Pushing the bag inside, he smirked, "Enjoy your gift."

Aris

Chapter 9

Aris had spent the last three months trying, failing, and trying again to be alone with Harlow. She always managed to avoid him. But then, just when he was about to give up, he'd catch her, the hazel eyes fixed on him, filled with a yearning that mirrored his own. Those eyes, sparkling with unshed tears, were far more expressive than she seemed to realize, the silence between them thick with unspoken words. Yet, a wall, cold and unforgiving, had risen between them, and he didn't know how to break through it, how to reach the woman who haunted his thoughts.

The next trial came in the form of his mother, a whirlwind of floral perfume and eager smiles, who seized every chance to parade eligible females from other covens before him. Each introduction was a brightly lit stage, the air thick with forced pleasantries. But almost all the prospects bored him within moments. Their laughter tinkled like fragile glass, their eyes gleaming with a superficial hunger that left him cold. They were vapid, shallow fang bangers, desperate to climb up the strongest male to get higher up in the echelons of their society. He tried explaining this to his mother, the words feeling like lead in his mouth as she dismissed his concerns with a gentle shush, insisting they came from good stock.

The sight of Harlow, radiant in the dim light, pulled his thoughts back to the looming ball, a swirling vortex of silks and hushed whispers in his mind's eye. A cold fist of fear clenched his gut, a sickening lurch. He fought it, a desperate internal struggle to shove the feeling away, to silence the pounding of his heart in his ears. This was it. He had been preparing for this his whole life; every fiber of his being trained for this moment. *This was the destiny chosen for me, and I need to go along with it, right? This is the life I would choose, right?*

His eyes stayed focused on Harlow. *Would she fight me, fight this, less after I turn?* The question swirled in his mind for a few minutes. *She will probably fight either way.*

His eyes devoured her as she glided through the ballroom. Her lithe figure moved with poised grace, each gesture radiating delicate confidence. The gentle sway of her hips accentuated her curves, a subtle rhythm that drew his gaze. He watched as she occasionally brushed a strand of her chocolate brown hair from her face, a soft, fleeting motion.

He couldn't explain the feeling, couldn't even sketch the hazy image in his mind, but the sight of her sparked something deep within himself. A nervous flutter tickled his stomach as he imagined their lives intertwined. He grew anxious, a tightness in his chest, desperate to make her see the vibrant future they could build together if she quit fighting.

His mind drifted back to what was going to happen in two weeks, and a knot formed anew in his stomach. *Maybe if I could get closer to my past, I could accept the future chosen for me. Fat chance either of my parents will tell me the truth though.*

The cool touch of a small hand landed gently on his arm. He glanced down at the perfectly manicured hand, the crimson polish gleaming under the chandeliers, and found Alena's expectant gaze. The faint, cloyingly sweet scent of her perfume filled his nostrils as he sighed inwardly. He wondered how many more polite rejections he could offer before his patience snapped and was replaced by outright rudeness.

A small cool hand touched his arm gently. Looking down he saw it belonged to Alena. He didn't know how many more nice ways he could explain no to her before he got out right rude.

"Hello, handsome," Alena cooed.

His mother's voice echoed in his mind, a soft reprimand. He remembered her instructing him to be polite to Alena, a woman neither of them cared for. A flicker of satisfaction had warmed him, the subtle victory of hearing his mother admit her dislike. But the subsequent lecture about being one of the heads of their coven, the need for a united front, whether or not they liked it, had been frustrating. He'd curtly agreed, promising to do his duty, the words tasting like ash.

"I have a meeting and can't talk right now," he shrugged.

"I know you are waiting for the stray." Alena flicked a hand towards Harlow. "But since you are paying her, she can wait to discuss the ball details. I wanted to see if you had a date for—"

"I'm going stag," he said, cutting her off.

"You realize you don't have to go stag," Alena sighed dramatically.

He looked at her, watching the way she batted her blue eyes, and felt nothing but disgust. "Go talk to my mother about who I should date. She seems to know who is best for me the way she keeps parading all you fang bangers around."

"Excuse me?" Her blue eyes grew wide.

"I mean, the best way to get in my pants and climb the social ladder here is to talk my mom into

liking you." His chilly green eyes locked with hers. *Apparently, it's today I ran out of nice things to say.* "She should be in her office. You can set up an appointment on her social calendar for when you want to be paraded in front of me."

"You're kidding, right?" Her eyes had turned a chilling shade of blue.

"Yes," he exhaled, rolling his eyes. "I am going stag. So, no dates allowed."

"Oh, you," she laughed, swatting his chest, "are just so funny. Well, maybe after the party we can... hang out."

"My mother has planned my entire night, so I am not sure that will happen."

"You don't think you can carve out a little time for me? You know a fang banger," she giggled like it was some inside joke between them.

Laughing sardonically, he replied. "I highly doubt my mother has any seconds left on the itinerary. Even down to my last and first feast."

"Well, maybe the next night we can go out on a date," she said, batting her eyes anew.

"I don't know if I can be seen with a..." he lowered his voice deceptively. "A fang banger." He smiled a smile that did not reach his eyes.

"Always the jokester," she giggled.

"I try," he said, winking before his eyes went back to his target.

"This party is the social event of the year, you know that, right?" Alena sighed. "Which means you need to ensure the right people see you. I had my dress

custom-made just for the occasion."

"Yes, so my mother had told me a million times," he said, trying to keep his voice steady. "I'm sure you spent a pretty penny on the dress."

"I am glad we are on the same page," Alena stated, seeming to be oblivious to the undercurrents he was giving. "Plus, what do I care what it costs?"

"As you shouldn't," he snorted, closing his eyes so she would not see his need to roll them.

"Maybe once you have been christened," she sighed. "You can work to eliminate the strays in the community. They really don't belong."

"Please excuse me; I have things to discuss." He bit his tongue to keep from retorting something far worse than he had before. He knew his mother would be upset if she knew he had *joked* like he did already. *But once I am christened, as she called it, I am far more likely to get rid of her than Harlow.*

Harlow

Chapter 10: Harlow

Harlow had spent the last three months dodging Aris, a self-imposed exile that left her feeling wretched. The mere sight of his blonde head across the room made her pulse thunder in her ears, a frantic drumbeat, yet she steeled herself and forced herself to run in the opposite direction. The memory of his woodsy cologne seemed to linger in her nostrils. He infuriated her, a burning ember of annoyance, and he captivated her, a mesmerizing flame she couldn't resist.

The purse he'd gifted her swung gently from her arm. She had gone to Hexquisite Hems; the price tag had screamed at her: $9,000.00. A wave of nausea had hit her then. She wanted to summon the anger, to despise the gesture, despise him, but all she felt was… complicity? Now, her fingers traced the cool, smooth texture of the faux Cetus scale. The vibrant scales shimmered, catching the light, morphing from emerald green to deep sapphire blue to rich amethyst purple.

The vintage doctor's bag shape felt surprisingly natural in her grip. When Alena saw the bag, her voice dripped with disdain as she asked where someone like Harlow could get such a thing. A smug satisfaction had bloomed within

Harlow as she simply shrugged and named the store.

The weight of the looming deadline pressed on her - two weeks to complete everything. She had just finished the walk-through with the rental company representative. Her eyes scanned the checklist, each item a sharp visual reminder of the tasks ahead for the day.

[] ~~Run through placement for table and chairs~~

[] Double check linens arrived

[] Check with Desi at Magickal Morsels for food orders

[] Message rep at Onyx to verify delivery time of blood

[] Verify staff and send training curriculum

Then there is the most important item I can't write on the list. Avoid Aris. After he had made her climax, she had wanted to taste him, his blood, and his skin. It had taken every cell in her body not to do it. Never once had he ever acted fearfully towards her, even then. He had been so calm. *Does he not under-stand that I am a monster?*

Her breath hitched as a warm hand, smelling faintly of sage and citrus, slid onto the small of her back. Before she turned, the familiar electricity spark-ing against her skin told her who it was. Looking up into his eyes, pools of deep forest green framed by dark lashes, she tried to fight the magnetic pull. His hand tightened, a gentle but firm pressure pulling her back into his orbit.

"Don't worry; your party will be magical," Harlow grumbled. Her eyes darted around trying to find an escape route.

His lips were a whispery touch against her lobe as he said, "Apart from those hazel eyes, do you know what else is magical?"

"What?" she murmured, feeling the warmth of those fingers gently applying pressure on her back.

"My fingers and tongue," he muttered, his warm breath fluttering against her neck. "Just let me know when you'd like to feel them again."

Her resolve crumbled, and she turned, her gaze meeting his. The subtle scent of mint, cool and sharp, wafted from his breath as she inhaled. A magnetic pull drew her closer, her body subtly shifting towards him. Her hand, hesitantly reaching out, pressed against the solid wall of his chest, and then she felt it—a steady, rhythmic thrum beneath her palm. His heartbeat. A human heartbeat. The realization jolted through her like an electric shock. With a gasp, as if scorched by an invisible flame, she recoiled and fled the room.

The rhythmic slap of her flats echoed against the marble as she sprinted down the hallway, her breath catching in her throat. She burst into the cool, tiled bathroom, the door clicking shut behind her with a soft thud. The scent of clean soap hung in the air. Her hands, clammy and trembling, found purchase on the smooth, cool porcelain of the sink. She closed her eyes, drawing in shaky, deep breaths, the air whistling softly in her ears as she exhaled slowly.

What is wrong with me? If I am not careful, I'll do to him what they did to me.

The air, cool against her flushed cheeks, filled her lungs as she inhaled deeply. With each steady

breath, the frantic drumming in her chest quieted. Looking at herself in the mirror, she murmured. "You can do this; all you need to do is avoid him until the party's over. I am done here for the evening and can go home." Smoothing her hair down, she smiled the closest thing to a cheerful face she could muster. "He's one male. There is no reason for me to act like a ninny over him."

She turned the knob, swinging the door inward. There he was, a silhouette framed against the fading light, and a smirk played on his lips. "So, you like the purse?"

After slamming the door shut, she stood there staring at it as boisterous laughter came from the other side. "Why do you keep trying to run from me?"

"I'm not running," she grumbled. Closing her eyes, she knew her voice did not hold conviction for the lie she told.

"You really should stop hiding from me and your feelings."

The rhythmic tap of his shoes faded as he walked away. She pushed open the door. Her heart, a tangled knot of longing and resolve, ached. A phantom image of him lingered in her mind's eye, but she knew, with a painful certainty, that she had to set him free.

Harlow took her time preparing for the evening,

anticipation buzzing in the air. She had hunted for the perfect white dress the week before. The fabric, a cool, sleek silk, hugged her figure, a gentle pressure against her skin, while modestly covering most of her skin. The high neckline, a soft caress against her throat, clung to her curves before cascading into a mermaid skirt that whispered against the floor as she moved. A daring open back dipped low, a cool breeze teasing her skin. Catching her reflection, she felt pretty. The brush, a familiar weight in her hand, glided through her hair. Debating whether to pin it up or let it fall, she sighed, the sound barely audible. Finally, she walked away, the weight of her hair a comforting presence against her back.

"You're overthinking things again," she mumbled.

Shadow leaped onto the comforter with a soft thump. His gentle mew, a delicate chime, echoed in the quiet room, signaling his desire for attention. She ran a hand over his back, feeling the slightly coarse texture of his fur beneath her fingertips.

"I think you are the only one who actually hears me."

Tawny eyes glaring at her and a slight tilt of the head were the only response she got.

"Maybe I need to go on a date, so I won't keep thinking about some spoiled rich boy."

Shadow pressed against her hand as he walked away.

"What's that line about getting over one guy you have to get under another?"

With a long, gusty exhale, she plopped onto the bed; the springs sighing softly beneath her weight. Next to her, Shadow's eyes, pools of liquid amber, met hers with a knowing look, a silent understanding passing between them in the quiet room.

"His family hates me. I need to forget him. He's not Romeo, and I sure as hell am not Juliet."

Pushing up, she walked back to the mirror. "Maybe he is more like Romeo, but I could never compete with a Juliet."

She glanced up and down her skinny frame. "I don't have huge breasts. Fuck, I'm barely a B cup. I'm covered in freckles from head to toe. Since turning and never getting sunlight for some reason, my freckles look even darker on my pale skin." Feeling self-conscious, she looked away from the mirror. "Maybe I'm more Heathcliff and he's Catherine."

The velvety rasp of Shadow's tongue echoed softly as he groomed his paw, his dark eyes locking onto hers. A silent, weighty question seemed to hang in the air, a visual puzzle she strained to piece together, the feeling of frustration itching at the back of her mind.

"I probably should stop beating myself up and just go do my job, right?"

Johnna Dee

Weave Your Dreams, Brew Your Magic in

Rusthollow

Aris

Chapter 11

Aris adjusted his red tie, the silky fabric gliding through his fingers. His parents had gifted him a brand-new suit, a luxurious red silk that matched his tie perfectly. Carefully, he inserted the ruby cufflinks into the red dress shirt. He ran his hand through his dirty blonde hair as his forest green eyes surveyed himself in the mirror.

As he stood there, nerves tightened their grip on him, threatening to consume him whole. The anticipation hung in the air, a palpable tension that made his heart race. Part of him longed for the night to be over, while another part yearned to escape and hide from the pain he knew was coming. This day, the culmination of his lifelong training, held a weight that was both exhilarating and terrifying.

He felt torn between his duties, his heart heavy with the conflicting emotions. As he stood there, a vivid picture of his human life played in his mind. The laughter of his friends echoed in his ears, the vibrant colors of the day danced before his eyes, and the comforting warmth of the sun kissed his skin, reminding him of the life he would soon leave behind. He would never see the sun again, feel its warmth. Despite all the preparation, his soul remained unready for the imminent and abrupt change that awaited him.

Harlow had meticulously organized every detail of tonight's Masquerade Ball, leaving nothing for him to do. So, he spent his last human day, staring mindlessly at his phone, bouncing between playing games and scrolling through PixelTome. The ball would start at 9 P.M. He had paid little attention to the plans, just let his mother and Harlow do whatever they wanted. Now he was unsure of what all they had planned for him tonight. He didn't even have the guest list. All he knew was that when the clock struck 10:09 P.M. tonight, Halloween night, the precise moment of his birth, that very moment would mark his transformation into his new life.

The bedroom door opened, and in walked the irresistible Harlow. Her luscious chocolate brown hair cascaded freely, swaying in sync with each swing of those hips. The aroma of her lilac perfume mingled in the air, adding a hint of allure to her already captivating presence. Her flawless ivory skin accentuated the darkness of her rose-red lips. Her tight white dress covered her from neck to toes, but clung to each curve. Despite his diligent search, he had yet to discover the faint scars left behind from her transformation. Her hazel eyes, filled with an enigmatic distance, scanned him without giving away any hint of her thoughts. Deciphering her had become a challenging endeavor these last two weeks, but he enjoyed trying to get under her skin.

"Everything is... Oh," she exclaimed as she approached him with her heels clicking on the white marble floors. "Your tie is crooked."

Her slender fingers delicately straightened the silk tie, the smooth fabric gliding effortlessly through her cool hands. As she finished, he gently placed his warm hand on top of hers. The drastic feel of the temperature difference between them always caught him off guard. With his lips curved into his most charming smile, he spoke, "Thank you, Harlow."

Her hazel eyes locked with his, captivating him in their depths. Flecks of green and gold danced within those irises, shimmering like scattered sunlight on a tranquil pond. A soft, barely audible sigh escaped her lips, causing his gaze to wander to her mouth. He noticed her teeth, which glistened in the light as they delicately grazed her plump bottom lip. Shaking her head, she stepped back as she pulled her hand away.

"Everything is ready for your arrival," her trembling voice said. Her eyes locked with his once again as her brow furrowed. Shaking her head, she turned as she sashayed out of the room, slamming the door as she left.

Laughing, he shook his head as he followed. Walking down the stairs, he tucked his hands into his pockets as he descended the stairs, the cocky grin on full display.

A triumphant smile slowly spread across his face as he realized he had gotten under her skin. Taking a deep breath, a surge of confidence washed through his veins. With his hands nestled in his pockets, he descended the stairs, each step echoing softly in the grand foyer. He could hear the live band playing as the music drifted throughout the house.

He confidently strode into the majestic ballroom; a cocky grin plastered on his face. The crystal chandelier sparkled, throwing rainbows across the crisp white linens adorning the tables that lined the edges of the ballroom. The faint scent of roses hung in the air as the centerpieces dripped with white roses. A lone table sat on the stage, showcasing a rich chocolate cake. He turned his eyes away, a subtle knot forming in his stomach, not wanting to study the stage too much.

The gazes of every attendee turned towards him, their eyes fixated. He couldn't help but notice the sea of creatures of the night, their ethereal forms draped in pristine white attire, numbering at least three dozen. A sudden shift in his demeanor occurred as the weight of their collective attention bore down upon him, causing his cockiness to waver, but his grin stayed in place.

As the crowd slowly parted, allowing a path to form, his mother gracefully stepped forward. Amara's sequined floor-length white dress shimmered under the lights. Her blonde hair, meticulously styled in a loose topknot, emphasized her pixie-ish face, each strand purposefully arranged. The twinkle in her blue eyes reflected love and adoration behind her white mask, illuminating the room as she beamed at him.

"There's my handsome lambkin!" she exclaimed as she cupped his cheeks.

His father, Tiberias, came up behind him, cuffing him gently on the shoulder. "There he is! I am so proud of you and can't wait for the hour of your turning."

"Thank you, Mother and Father," he said smoothly, with no hint of the nerves coursing through him. Years of diligent practice had honed his ability to maintain a steady heartbeat, a skill imperative when cohabiting with his family, who could discern his emotions merely by listening to the rhythmic thumping of his heart. Whether he was brimming with excitement, consumed by sadness, or experiencing any other intense emotion, the betraying pulse in his chest would inevitably give him away. "Everything looks perfect."

"Of course," Amara laughed. "Harlow followed all my instructions to a 'T'. I know this night will be perfect. We even got you a tasty treat from the bakery in town that you love, Magickal Morsels. This is your last meal, and I wanted to make it special."

"Perfect," Aris said as he gently pressed a kiss to his mother's forehead. "I can't wait to try some."

With his mother's comforting touch, she guided him towards the elevated platform adorned with a table

where the cake awaited and two posts with shackles attached to them stood behind the table. The air was thick as he took his seat, his smile fading as he realized the weight of the moment. A hushed silence fell over the room, the gazes of all in attendance fixated upon him, waiting. His eyes scanned the crowd, absorbing their expectant energy. The scent of freshly baked cake wafted to his nostrils—devil's food cake. His hands trembled slightly as his mother delicately sliced a generous piece of the confection, placing it before him. The weight of their collective gaze bore down upon him, intensifying the urge to run.

"What spell is in it?" Aris asked, eyeing his mother.

Laughing, Amara shook her head. "Maybe there is, maybe there isn't."

"Mother," Aris scolded playfully.

"Just a small spell of cheer." Amara replied with a wide grin.

I know this is part of the ceremony, but damned if I wish it weren't, he thought. *Maybe if I rush, I can get this over with and be done with all the eyes ogling me.*

Gazing up at his mother, a smile stretched across his face as he took a bite of the cake. The moment it touched his tongue; the velvety delight caused his taste buds to dance. He closed his eyes, shutting out the crowd, fully immersing himself in the blissful sensation. The roar of cheers from the onlookers filled the air as his pleasure faded. He quickly shoveled the morsels into his mouth, trying to put an end to the charade.

"Slow down and enjoy," his mother admonished.

Looking up at her, he whispered, "It's hard to

enjoy while everyone's watching and cheering."

Laughing, she stroked his cheek. "Slow down anyway."

Rolling his eyes, he slowed down.

He desperately tried to ignore the piercing gazes as he took each bite. With the last bite consumed, his eyes darted towards the massive clock on the back wall. The ticking seemed to grow louder than even the music playing, intensifying his unease. Twenty minutes remained until the commencement of the ritual, causing his stomach to churn. He wiped his face, then placed the napkin on the now-empty plate.

"Was it delicious?" his mother asked.

Nodding, he smiled warmly at her, his eyes filled with affection, as he gracefully rose from his seat. With gentle strength, he enveloped her in a tight bear hug. As he inhaled the delicate scent of her floral perfume, a thought crossed his mind - *what did my birth mother smell like?*

"You will remember this last meal always, my lambkin," she whispered. Her blue eyes shone with unshed tears as she fussed with his hair.

"Of course I will," he whispered back.

He knew his heart was racing, and no matter how much he tried to find his inner Zen; it was long gone.

"It only hurts for a moment."

"I got this, Mother."

"I know you do." She beamed up at him.

"Dance with me?"

"Of course."

He extended his warm hand towards his mother. With a gentle grip, she placed her delicate fingers in his, feeling the strength that lay within. The soft melody of the music filled the air as they moved across the polished dance floor. With each step, the subtle scent of fresh roses wafted through the room. Together, they glided gracefully, their feet barely making a sound. As the song ended, a firm hand gripped his shoulder.

"Come here, Aris," Tiberias said, pride dripping from his voice.

Tiberias's strong hand guided Aris to the stage.

Aris turned and glanced at his father. As his green eyes met Aris', they shimmered with a vibrant intensity, mirroring the same shade he saw when he peered at his own reflection. The similarities never failed to astonish him. The same angular jawline and high cheekbones only emphasized their resemblance, yet their differences were apparent also. While Tiberias stood at a solid 5'11, Aris towered over him at 6'2. His father had a stocky build, akin to that of a linebacker, while Aris possessed a lean muscularity.

"As the hour grows upon us, it is time to make one last wish," his father's voice boomed across the room, not needing a microphone.

Standing there, he tucked his hands into his pockets, feeling the cool fabric against his fingertips as he debated one last wish. Turning, he scanned the crowd, the murmurs of conversation filling his ears as he wrestled with the decision. Then his eyes locked on her, his heart quickening at the sight of her. Her white dress hugged her curves, accentuating her beauty as she stood at the back of the room, a tablet in hand as she was still working. A smirk spread across his face as the wish floated through his mind.

"A kiss," he said, turning back to his father.

"A kiss?" A knowing smirk came across his father's face.

"Yes."

"Whom shall you receive this kiss from?"

The crowd hushed as he paused dramatically. "Harlow Rathmore."

"What?" a high-pitched voice squeaked from the back of the room.

His father's brows furrowed as his lips turned down. "Are you sure this is what you want?"

He knew he had disappointed his father with his choice. She was not of their blood, but a stray that had been allowed to live on their lands. The disappointment hung heavy in the air, palpable like the tension before a storm. But that wouldn't stop him from getting what he wanted.

"Yes."

Johnna Dee

Damascus Coven

Aris

Chapter 12

Aris's eyes sparkled with anticipation as he turned his gaze towards Harlow, who stood at the back of the room. The murmuring crowd shifted, creating a pathway for her to step forward. Harlow's face flushed as she locked her intense gaze onto him.

"Well?" he asked as he smirked at her.

She stood there; a figure cloaked in anger. The heat emanating from her body seemed visible, like wisps of steam rising. With cautious steps, her hips swayed, casting a magnetic spell. His eyes leisurely traced her form, devouring every curve. Though he knew he shouldn't take pleasure in this sweet agony, he couldn't deny his enjoyment. As she took the stage, her presence filled the air, mingling with the intoxicating scent of her perfume that filled his nostrils. Her eyes burned with a fiery rage, yet he yearned for them to ignite with another kind of passion.

"Why are you doing this?" she whispered.

"You could say no." He raised an eyebrow at her.

His gaze fixed on her, captivated by the subtle movements of her jaw as it clenched and unclenched. He could almost hear the faint sound of her teeth grinding against one another. He waited patiently, wanting to know which word would slip past her lips.

"Whatever," she snorted.

"Is that a yes?"

"You know I can't say no to the prodigal son."

Laughing, disappointment washed through him. "You just need to say the word."

"I'll take the kiss!" a voice that sounded like Alena screamed.

"I'd take a smooch from you, Aris, any day!" Carolina shouted. He tried to hide his snicker since she was older than his mother.

"I called dibs first!" Alena growled.

"Let's just get this over with," Harlow grumbled.

She balanced delicately on the tips of her toes, her lips puckered. He hesitated, contemplating whether to turn away and exact the humiliation she had inflicted on him. But the desire to taste her again, which had consumed him since their first meeting, now surged through his veins. As he encircled her waist with his arm, he pulled her towards him, their bodies crashing in a collision of softness against hardness. In that instant, her eyes widened, and a gasp escaped from between her parted lips. With a gentle yet urgent motion, he pressed his lips against hers, his tongue gliding in, igniting a fire.

Pure heaven, he thought. *She tastes better than I remembered.*

The fiery intensity surged within him as he savored the exquisite taste of her. His fingertips gripped the velvety contours of her hips, sinking into their supple flesh. Tentatively, she trailed her hands along his chest, tracing a scorching path up to encircle his neck, leaving a trail of smoldering desire in their wake. With a sense of triumph, he caressed her backside, pressing her closer. His breath caught in his chest as he fought to stifle the urge to moan.

A soft cough echoed behind him, a gentle reminder that it was time to let her go because they were not alone. With a lingering taste on his tongue, he relished the last moment before reluctantly pulling away. As he gazed at her, her eyes slowly opened and showed a darkening desire and a primal hunger. Stepping back, he turned towards his father.

"It's time," Tiberias said.

In an instant, the fiery flames of desire transformed into a chilling apprehension that consumed him. The sight before him sent shivers down his spine. He had spent the night avoiding looking at them after his first glimpse, the cold metal chains glinting on the posts. Amplified by the eerie silence, his racing heartbeat echoed in his ears, a drumbeat he knew everyone could hear. Every nerve in his body trembled as he stood there, waiting for his veins to be drained.

Walking over, he stood between the tall posts. The metallic click of the shackles being fastened around his wrists filled the air, echoing in his ears. The cool touch of the metal sent a shiver down his spine, as if icy fingers were tracing his skin. Anxiety gnawed at his insides, twisting like a vise, making it difficult to breathe. Inhaling deeply, he caught the scent of his father's aftershave, but it did little to ease his racing heart. With practiced hands, his father loosened the silk tie around his neck. The top buttons of his shirt exposed a sliver of his bare chest to the cool breeze.

"It only hurts for a short while, alright?" Tiberias said sternly. "I won't ask if you're ready."

Nodding solemnly, Aris closed his eyes. The sound of his father's labored breathing filled the room as his father's fangs pierced his neck. A sharp, searing pain shot through him, causing his muscles to tense. Desperation surged within him as he strained against the unforgiving chains, their cold metal biting into his

wrists. The metallic scent of blood filled the air as his life drained from him. Chills ran down his spine, intensifying as his vision blurred and dimmed. A wave of dizziness washed over him, causing his legs to buckle beneath him. Despite his efforts to rise, his weakened legs betrayed him, leaving him suspended helplessly from his aching arms.

"You're doing good, lambkin," a female voice, sounding almost disembodied, said.

Something icy grabbed hold of his chin, sending a shiver down his spine. The frigid touch seeped into his body, leaving him numb and paralyzed. Desperate, he tried to resist the grip, straining to pry open his mouth, but his feeble attempt lacked any strength. A torrent of warm liquid trickled down his throat, its metallic taste instantly making him want to retch. As his stomach churned and revolted, he gagged, only to have his mouth forcibly closed. Suddenly, a scorching liquid fire ignited in his stomach, surging through his veins and consuming his entire being. His body convulsed, and with a jolt, his eyes snapped open. He desperately fought to rise, his face turning pale as the acidic taste surged up his throat.

"Stand up!" He heard the shout as if it was miles away, drifting into the fog of pain shooting through him.

He pushed up, but his knees buckled under the pain.

"Stand up, Aris!" The voice was louder this time.

As he desperately searched for the source of the piercing screams, his surroundings blurred into a dizzying whirl. Agonizing pain reverberated through every inch of his body, drowning out all other sensations.

"You are a Damascus, and you will not do this on

your knees!"

Struggling against the force, he exerted himself to rise, his body swaying unsteadily. His legs quivered, their weakness clear. Every muscle fought for peace as his body warred against the pain.

"That's my son." Someone grabbed his chin again. "Open up."

This time, he willingly parted his lips, allowing the liquid to cascade into his mouth. It flowed smoothly down, without triggering a retching reflex. The warm liquid, reminiscent of sweet nectar this time, flooded his senses, filling him up. As it coursed through his veins, the pain subsided, replaced by an overwhelming euphoria that slowly enveloped him.

Opening his eyes, the world around him transformed from a blurry haze to a crystal-clear vision. Every detail became vivid, as if he was witnessing everything in high definition for the first time. The colors that surrounded him seemed to intensify, radiating with brightness and vibrancy. The surrounding sounds became heightened also, each one distinct and clear. He could even discern the faint rustle of fabric from a servant upstairs.

His father patted him on the shoulder, smiling brightly. "You are officially one of us now, boy. Or should I say, man? I am so proud of you, Aris."

Smiling, he shook his wrists; the shackles clanked. Nodding, his father got the hint and unlocked them. Rubbing his wrists, he watched as the red marks from the shackles slowly faded away.

He had never felt more alive than he did at this moment. He could not for the life of him figure out why he had been so scared of this day. Looking around the crowd, his eyes stopped on her. He waited patiently

for her to look at him. It didn't take long for her eyes to be locked on him; she was nibbling her lip. Her brow furrowed as worry darkened her hazel eyes. He smiled at her and winked.

His attention drew back to his father as he stepped forward to speak. "I would like to reintroduce everyone to my son, my heir, and the newest member of our coven, Aris Damascus."

Johnna Dee

Damascus

Coven

Harlow

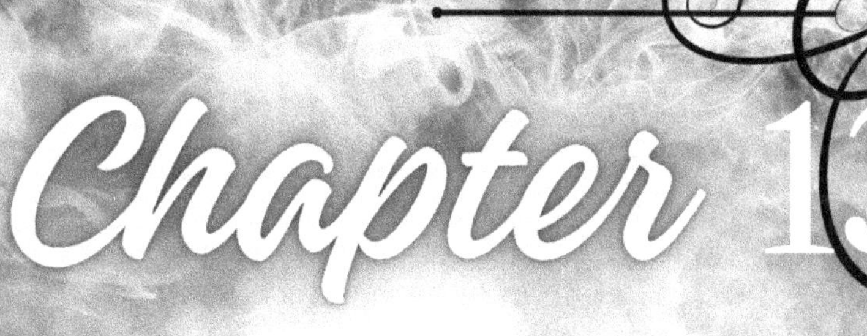

Chapter 13

Harlow's gaze lifted; her eyes fixed on the stage. As Aris locked eyes with her, a rush of crimson embarrassment flooded her cheeks, making her skin tingle. Anxiously, she fidgeted, attempting to conceal herself behind another partygoer, their raucous cheers filling the air. But her efforts were futile, as the bustling crowd shifted, and Aris confidently strode towards her. Those mesmerizing green eyes never wavered, holding her captive, their magnetic pull impossible to resist. Though she yearned to avert her gaze, its enchanting allure drew her further into his spell.

"Dance with me," he stated, holding his hand out to her.

The bile rose in her throat, a bitter taste, as rage warred with nausea and a desperate urge to flee. But she was rooted, trapped. Her small hand, swallowed by his large, rough one, felt the calluses dig slightly. The violins soared, a sweet, aching sound, as he pulled her onto the polished dance floor. His chest, a warm, hard wall, pressed against her, her heart beating a frantic rhythm.

"You smell delicious," he murmured, his breath warm against her skin as his nose brushed her neck.

Hesitantly, she replied, "Thank you." She hesitated before speaking again. "Why me?"

"You know why. I know you feel that pull too."

Her mind swirled as he twirled her

across the polished floor; the varnish gleaming under the chandelier's bright light. For a moment, the music faded as she closed her eyes; the world dissolved at the touch of his embrace. Her head nestled against his chest, the steady thump of his heart a comforting rhythm against her ear. The waltz flowed effortlessly, their steps a silent conversation on the smooth wood. She inhaled deeply, the coppery tang of blood, his and his father's, sharp and metallic in the air. His hand, strong and sure, rested at the small of her back. She leaned into him, craving the firm pressure of his body against hers. Months of resistance crumbled; she surrendered to the feel of his touch, the ghost of his breath on her skin, and the strength radiating from him.

I can go back to fighting after this dance; for now, I am just going to give in.

The final note faded, a lingering sweetness in the air, as his mother's hand closed warmly around his arm. He glanced back at her, green eyes smoldering. "I'll be back."

She watched him retreat, catching the glint of red silk on his retreating back. A faint, lingering scent of his cologne hung in the air, a ghost of his presence. Turning, she went back to her duties. She rushed around, a whirlwind of motion, her eyes darting back to him, catching glimpses of his amused smile. Time blurred into a hazy rush of sounds and movement: the clinking of glasses, hushed conversations, a low thrum of music. Then, a sickening lurch—he was gone. She swallowed the bitter taste of disappointment, the tightness in her chest, a physical ache, as she walked towards the bar, the polished wood cool under her hand.

A strong hand closed around her arm, familiar and warm, spinning her around. "Let's go," he whispered as his hand gripped hers.

A torrent of thoughts raced through her mind,

overwhelming her senses. Despite herself, her hand succumbed to his firm grasp, their fingers intertwining. As he pulled her along, the murmurs of the crowd echoed in her ears, their gaze fixated on them. The burning sensation on her cheeks intensified, but she willed herself to ignore the prying eyes, focusing on his powerful pull through the sea of onlookers. The weight of their stares felt suffocating, making her yearn for escape. Finally, as they stepped out of the ballroom, a wave of relief washed over her, freeing her from the scrutiny. Glancing back, she noticed envious eyes still locked on her, their gaze filled with a mix of longing and resentment. One set of baby blues seemed to burn hotter as she locked eyes with Alena. Her feet faltered as they reached the first step, her apprehension mingling with a strange flutter in her stomach, an intoxicating blend of fear and anticipation. She knew she should break free, walk away, and never return, but her hand remained nestled in his, her feet obediently following his lead.

"Where are you taking me?" she asked breathlessly.

He threw a smirk over his shoulder as he continued up the stairs.

Even though she knew the answer, a part of her wanted him to say anywhere else but where she knew they were heading. As they drew nearer to his bedroom, her stomach fluttered, sending a wave of nervousness throughout her body. The opulent surroundings faded from her awareness; her focus solely fixated on the pristine white door ahead.

With a forceful push, he swung the door open, creating a whirlwind of emotions within her. The pounding of her heart echoed in her ears as her mind became flooded with a torrent of thoughts. A lump formed in her throat, making it difficult to swallow. As they entered, her feet hesitated, refusing to budge any further. In response, he turned his gaze towards her, those piercing eyes staring a hole into her heart.

"Don't get timid on me now, Harlow," he murmured.

"I..." she started as the words lodged in her throat.

His hand, once warm, now sent a chill through her as it came up and gently caressed her cheek. Part of her missed the warmth of his touch from before he turned. That touch sent a shiver down her spine, a mix of eager anticipation and underlying fear warring within her. She could almost hear the sound of her own heartbeat pounding in her ears, the only sound besides their breathing. The cool touch of his hand slid down her neck, igniting a fiery sensation that spread like wildfire. Nervously, her tongue flicked across her fangs. With a slow, deliberate movement, his hand traveled to her collarbone, tracing a path of electrifying sensations. As it ventured further down, reaching the crest of her breast, she couldn't help but inhale deeply, taking in the intoxicating scent of his cologne. The pressure of his hand increased, pressing harder into her delicate flesh, causing a mix of pleasure and a hint of pain that heightened her senses.

Her eyes locked intently with his, their gazes entwined in a magnetic connection that held her captive. His hand glided sensuously downwards. As his touch journeyed past her nipple, it puckered up in response to his gentle caress. Moving further down, his hand settled on her stomach before gracefully sliding around her waist. Suddenly, he spun her around, causing her head to spin in sync with the swift motion as she now faced away from him. Before her, the grand four-poster bed towered, casting an imposing presence in the room. His hands expertly found their way to the

center of her back. With a swift tug, the zipper obediently glided down, unleashing a wave of anticipation
within her. The smooth white silk cascaded down her
torso, slipping past her legs until it gracefully pooled at
her feet. Standing there, adorned only in delicate white
lace panties and vibrant red heels, she could feel his
breath, warm and inviting, caressing her neck, height-
ening her senses.

His nose nuzzled the back of her neck. "I can
practically taste the blood pumping through your
veins."

"You're freshly turned. You'll get used to that
one day," she mumbled.

His serpentine tongue flicked across her delicate
neck, sending shivers down her spine. Goosebumps
erupted across her back. Sliding slowly, his tongue
reached her shoulder, followed by the sharp intrusion
of his fangs piercing her tender flesh. In a forceful
motion, he pulled her body against his unyielding form.
The mingling aroma of her blood intertwined with the
alluring citrusy notes of his cologne engulfed her senses, intoxicating and overwhelming her.

"Not too much," she whispered as her head
spun.

As he persistently drank her essence, she swiftly
jabbed her elbow into his side. The force of her blow
elicited a guttural grunt to escape his lips as he released
her.

"That's enough," she growled, stepping away.

She felt an itch as her wound slowly began
to heal. Turning swiftly, she looked at him. His eyes,
glazed over and distant, remained fixed on her, their
intensity unsettling. His once pristine red suit was now
saturated with a macabre mixture of her blood, his fa-

ther's, and his own, forming a grotesque tableau. With a swift motion, his hand rose to his chin, smearing the blood across his face.

"Was I too rough, my little delicacy?" he murmured.

She shook her head, still feeling a little light-headed.

His cocky grin spread across his face, revealing a flash of pearly white teeth covered in blood. His eyes, filled with a mischievous glimmer, slowly traveled up and down her body like a feather-light caress. The intensity of his gaze made her feel both desired and vulnerable, as if he hungered to consume every ounce of her being. A primal urge to flee surged through her, but her feet remained firmly planted, unable to escape the magnetic pull of his presence. The look he bestowed upon her was a potent blend of desire and a promise to savor every drop of her existence. It was a look that both thrilled and terrified her.

Closing the distance between them, he crashed his mouth onto hers with a force that ignited a symphony of sensations. Their lips collided, creating a tumultuous collision as his tongue invaded her mouth. She tasted the tang of her life's nectar on his lips, a bittersweet flavor that sent shivers through her soul. The taste filled her mouth as his tongue danced and swirled, an intoxicating rhythm that left her breathless. Simultaneously, his hands reached down and gripped the supple curves of her ass, drawing her closer to him. With a gentle lift, she found herself standing on tiptoes, her body pressed against his. The hard, undeniable presence of his arousal met the softness of her core, causing a soft moan to escape her lips.

Her hands instinctively sought solace in the tangle of his hair, fingers gripping tightly and tugging in a desperate attempt to anchor herself in the whirlwind

of desire.

As his lips parted from hers, a sense of emptiness washed over her, yearning for the taste that once filled her mouth. Slowly, his mouth traced a path down her chin, his moist tongue gliding along her neck, sending shivers down to the pit of her core. The newfound sharpness of his fangs delicately grazed her tender skin, evoking a mix of pleasure and anticipation.

In a hushed tone, he whispered, "Gods," as his lips caressed her throat, the gentle scrape of his fangs intensifying the sensation. "I crave to drink every drop of you, to explore and taste every inch of you."

"Aris," she uttered, half in protest and half in request.

"Yes?" he breathed as his mouth went further down.

His breath feathered across her skin before he sank his teeth into the flesh of her breast. Anticipating the bittersweet pain of his teeth piercing her flesh, she braced herself, but it never came. Instead, his mouth descended, capturing her taut nipple. The scrape of his teeth against her sensitive flesh as the sensations danced between pleasure and pain before he released it.

He delicately nibbled his way down her stomach, each movement sending a shiver through her body. He stopped at her core as she felt his breath through the lace. His hands gripped the sides of her panties, sliding them effortlessly down, his fingertips tracing a tantalizing path down her legs. As her eyes lowered, she watched the top of his head, his tousled dirty blonde hair inviting her touch. Her own hands reached out, entangling themselves in the soft waves, adding to the sensory symphony unfolding. His hands glided back up her legs, their gentle touch coaxing her to open herself up to him. With a deep inhale, he took in the scent of her desire. His tongue flicked out, unleashing a torrent of pleasure coursing through her entire being. A surge of intensity tightened her core as he sucked her clit into his mouth, intensifying the sensations beyond her wildest dreams.

As the pressure built in her core, his tongue continued to dance across her clit. Feelings she had not experienced since she had been human raced through her blood as he explored her core. Her legs trembled as her fingers dug into his scalp to steady herself. His hands slid across to her ass to help steady her. The pressure was building inside her until it was about to explode, but then he stopped.

Glancing downward, her eyes were drawn to the mischievous glimmer dancing in his eyes, accompanied by the sound of a slow, satisfied chuckle escaping his lips. She was torn between the urge to push him away and the tantalizing thought of burying his face between her thighs again.

"I just need another taste," he whispered.

Her gaze fixed on him, her brow furrowing as she observed him tracing his tongue across his teeth, showcasing his newly formed fangs. With a wide-open mouth, he swiftly sank his teeth into her thigh, eliciting a mixture of pain and bliss. A torrent of sensations coursed through her, as she could almost taste the metallic tang of her own essence and feel the warm trickle of her life force being consumed by him.

Her head spun, the world blurring around her like a whirlwind. In a desperate grip, she clutched his hair; the strands sliding between her trembling fingers. With a firm tug, she pulled his head back, her blood dripping from his chin. As her eyes met his misty green gaze, a surge of electricity sparked between them. Muttering, she said, "Enough, please."

His rough, wet tongue eagerly lapped up the warm, metallic-scented blood that slowly trickled down her thigh. The rhythmic motion of his tongue as he lapped up her blood creating an intoxicating symphony of pleasure. The itchiness that accompanied her healing wound merged with the electric currents of desire coursing through her veins. As he rose to his feet, a sense of emptiness engulfed her, aching for more of his touch, craving his tongue, yearning for the completeness that only he could provide.

His eyes, glazed with intoxication, greedily drank in the sight of her. In their depths, she could still see the fiery hunger for bloodlust burning. Holding her breath, she trembled beneath the piercing gaze of his emerald eyes. Time seemed to stretch endlessly as she anxiously awaited his next move. A shiver ran down her spine under the intense scrutiny, her skin prickling with anticipation.

After what felt like an eternity, he stood. His hands reached for her as he lifted her; he cradled her in his arms. Carrying her towards the bed, he deposited her on it unceremoniously. Pressing himself against her, she felt the length of him. The damp silk of his suit clung to her, cool against her skin, as his mouth crashed down upon hers. In a symphony of desperation, his lips devoured her with an insatiable hunger.

Her hands desperately clawed at the delicate silk fabric, yearning to feel his skin against hers. His hands, like skilled explorers, traversed all over her body, leaving a trail of tingling sensations in their wake. The fabric of her being unraveled as his fingers delved deep inside her, causing her hips to instinctively buck in pleasure. She could feel the mounting pressure in her core, like a coiled spring ready to unleash. His fingers pressed deeper and faster. Labored breaths escaped her lips as she fought to maintain a semblance of control, but it slipped through her fingers, leaving her powerless in the waves of ecstasy flowing through her. Her breath trapped in her throat as the world spun out of control.

Her body eased into a state of relaxation as her mind drifted away on a sea of tranquility. The faint sound of a zipper reached her ears. In a swift motion, his rigid shaft found its place at her entrance, hovering for a moment before filling her completely. A gasp escaped her lips. Pulling at his jacket and shirt, she reveled in the sensation of his skin beneath her fingertips as her nails dug in, leaving indented marks in their wake. Her nose brushed against his chin. Unable to contain her desire, she sank her fangs into the flesh of his neck, savoring the intoxicating sweetness of his essence. His blood, pristine and invigorating, carried a subtle hint of chocolate. As his thrusts intensified, the rush of blood surged through her veins, prompting her to retract her teeth. A euphoric sensation enveloped her, her mind floating amidst the pleasure building, while her body tightened like a taut bowstring.

Her back arched in a graceful curve. With each desperate attempt to take him deeper, her senses became consumed by the overwhelming pleasure, blurring the memory of just a moment ago. Waves of ecstasy crashed over her, engulfing her in a symphony of sensations. Fingers tightly clutched at him, as if he were a lifeboat amidst a tempestuous sea, her only salvation. The mounting pressure intensified, reaching its crescendo, and then exploded once more, leaving her breathless. His groan of pleasure reverberated through the air, blending with the sounds of their entangled bodies. In this intoxicating haze, the world spun around her, a whirlwind of bliss covered in blood.

Harlow looked at Aris, sleeping peacefully next to her. The clock on the nightstand told her it was an hour till daybreak. With a warmth spreading in her heart before doubt crept in, the war started internally. *This is so wrong. I have been alive for a century, and he has been alive for twenty-one years. He has barely any life experience. Plus, he would probably be shamed for being with me, a stray.*

Along with doubt, fear crept in. Gently getting up, she walked over to where her dress was and pulled it on. She refused to look at him, scared her resolve would break if she looked back even once.

Walking into the bedroom's ensuite bathroom, she splashed water on her face to clean up the blood. As she left the bathroom, her eyes lighted on him on the bed. His chin was stained crimson with her blood. Her hands itched to wipe it away and to brush the stray lock off his forehead. Shaking her head, she turned away, walking out the bedroom door.

As she stepped out onto the landing, Amara stood there. A sweetly sad smile on her face. "Nice to see you again, Harlow."

"Nice to see you, Amara," Harlow whispered, her eyes downcast.

Amara let out a dramatic sigh. "I hate to be the

bearer of bad news, but I feel I must." Amara paused.

Harlow swallowed hard, the metallic tang of anxiety coating her tongue. A faint creak echoed from the rafters above, a sound that tightened the knot in her stomach. She wanted to lift her eyes, to face whatever awaited her, but the courage remained elusive.

Amara continued, "He is young, and I think the problem was you played hard to get, and I encouraged you to."

Her breath caught in her throat, words failing her as a crimson blush, hot as her memory of a summer's sun, painted her cheeks.

"You have been around long enough to know he will grow bored once he has caught you, if you may," Amara's voice, sharp and clear. "For your own sake, I suggest you cut him off before you get too invested. You may not understand, but I am trying to do what's best for my son and for you. Even if you convinced him to have a relationship with you, it would never work out. He is a leader; he has been trained from birth to help lead our coven. He is strong, brave and loyal. Where you on the other hand." Amara flicked a graceful hand at Harlow. "Have no coven, no loyalties. You leave places on whatever whim you decide. I researched you and saw you never stay in one place too long. You would just bring him down, especially when you leave like you inevitably will."

"You're right," Harlow murmured, feeling every fiber of her being vibrating with shame and sadness. "I need to leave before the sun comes up. It's obvious I don't belong here."

Amara said nothing else, the rhythmic click of her high heels against the polished floor growing fainter as she walked away, leaving a lingering sense of unease hanging in the air.

Johnna Dee

Damascus Coven

Aris

Chapter 14

Aris jolted awake, the lingering tang of her blood still ghosting on his tongue, her presence a warm echo in his heart. He stretched, the linen cool beneath his fingertips, and registered the empty space beside him. The silence of the room pressed in as he rose, padding towards the bathroom, expecting to hear the rush of water. But the room was still and vacant. He pulled on a pair of sweatpants, ignoring the dried blood clinging to his skin, and stepped out of the room.

He walked around the darkened house; the shadows clinging to the corners of his vision, the murmur of voices drawing him like a moth to a flickering flame. He descended the creaking stairs to his father's office. As he neared, the voices ceased, swallowed by a sudden silence, but beneath it, a frantic drumbeat pulsed in his ears—the heavy thud of hearts racing in the stillness.

"Oh, for fuck's sake, Aris," Tiberias laughed. "Can you clean up and look presentable before you run around the house? The last thing we need is the staff gossiping."

"Lambkin." Amara shook her head. "I washed your face at the ball, and now I have to wash your face again. People will think you're a heathen."

"Let them think it," Aris shrugged.

Amara spat onto the worn cotton of her handkerchief. She balled the cloth in her fist and walked towards him.

"Nope," Aris shook his head, backing away. He held his hand up hoping to ward his mother away. "Not happening. I will go take a shower as soon as you answer one question."

Tiberias bellowed, his laughter echoing off the walls. "Leave the boy be," he gasped out between guffaws.

Sighing, Amara stopped approaching him. "What's your question?"

"Did you see where Harlow scurried off to?" Aris smiled, eyeing his mother, knowing she might at any second come at him with the spit rag.

Shaking his head, Tiberias replied, "Did not see her at all after the party."

Aris's gaze snagged on his mom, his eyes following her every move as Amara pointedly averted her own, feigning interest in a painting.

"Mom?" Aris asked.

Exhaling deeply, she turned back to look at Aris. "She said something about wanting to leave."

"That's it?" Aris's brow furrowed, a deep line etching itself between his eyebrows as he squinted.

Aris's eyes narrowed, the soft crinkle of his brow a silent question as he watched his mother. She chewed her lip, a nervous habit he knew well. Amara's eyes, bright with an anxiety he could almost taste, darted to Tiberias before returning to him, her gaze a tangible weight.

"Mother," Aris whispered in a deep, serious tone.

"She said she needed to leave before the sun

came up because she doesn't belong here."

"Alright," Aris frowned. "That's it?"

"Umm," Amara stuttered. "Yes."

"I am going to go get her and drag her back." Aris's voice cracked with a desperate edge. He raked his fingers roughly through his hair, the strands whispering against each other as they escaped his grasp.

"Boy!" Tiberias exclaimed, all laughter gone from his voice. "You're a mess, and you can't leave while the sun is out."

Aris's eyes, wide and a little panicked, darted between his parents. The low hum of their disapproval felt like a tightening in his chest as he remembered he could no longer come and go as he pleased. Nodding quickly, he turned, the floorboards creaking softly underfoot as he retreated upstairs.

He jumped into the shower, the sudden rush of hot water a welcome sting against his cool skin. The metallic scent of blood filled the steamy air as the water ran crimson down the drain. He wrapped a thick, fluffy towel around his waist and headed to his walk-in closet to get dressed.

"Lambkin," Amara murmured from behind him.

Whirling around, the sudden movement made his head swim momentarily, while he stared at her. The sight of her silhouette against the dim hallway light caught him off guard. He hadn't heard the soft whisper of her footsteps approaching or the gentle click of the door as she entered his room.

"We need to talk," Amara stated calmly.

"I'm not up for a lecture," Aris snorted.

"I'm not here to lecture," Amara started. She walked over to the closet and started going through his clothes. "Harlow is not—"

"Didn't you just say you weren't here to lecture me?" he interrupted her. He leaned against the door-jamb. His skin felt slick and damp against the wood, beads of water catching the light like tiny diamonds.

"I'm not."

"Then don't explain to me what type of woman is right or wrong for me."

"I need you to listen to me carefully."

"So, it is a lecture?" He grabbed the pants she handed him and tossed them on the floor. Pulling a random pair of slacks out instead. *I don't care what I wear; I just need her to understand I have a mind and heart of my own.* "Let me start the lecture then. You remember all the stories you told me about yours and Dad's relationship?"

"Of course I do, but that—"

Interrupting her again, he continued, "You spoke about how your sires constantly told you how he was wrong, and he would never be good for you. You disregarded them and followed your heart. That led to disruption and internal conflict within the coven. In the end, you and Dad took over and have ruled the coven since. Would you give up following your heart? Even knowing all the struggles, you went through, would you go back in time and choose another mate?"

"No," she whispered.

"So, before you start that lecture, answer one question. Should I follow my heart or blindly obey your decisions?"

"Your heart," she sighed, her shoulders sagging. "I am your mother, and I'm trying to guide you on the right path, is all."

"I know." He nodded.

"I want what's best for you, and I worry you are not on the right path."

"What's best for me is to follow my heart, and my heart says..." The air hung still and heavy, the only sound the distant chirping of unseen crickets. He paused, a sudden wave of realization washing over him. He'd been chasing her, blindly running, a frantic race towards a shimmering mirage, never questioning what or why he was running. Now, in the quiet stillness, a faint understanding bloomed. He felt a warmth spread through his chest, a subtle recognition of the unspoken bond between them, something profound he couldn't quite grasp, yet knew was undeniably special. "She's the one."

"I am sorry," she whispered, her voice ringing with truth and sadness. "I was trying to do what I thought was best and not looking at the man, you were becoming."

Smiling at his mother, he murmured, "I would forgive you anything."

"That's good to know," she said, coming up and cupping his cheeks. "Now get dressed, my lambkin. You were my heart from the first day they put you in my arms. As I cradled you as a baby, I knew I would do whatever it took to take care of you. I guess that means now backing off and letting you do what you feel is right. I love you."

"I love you, too, Mom." He brushed his lips across her forehead.

Damascus Coven

The last couple of hours before sunset crawled by each minute an eternity. Aris, restless, wore a path in the floor, the creaks of the wood a constant rhythm to his anxiety. Finally, as the last sliver of sun dipped below the horizon, he bolted, the cool evening air rushing against his face as he sped towards Harlow's place.

He rapped his knuckles against the aged oak and waited. Each tick of an unseen clock seemed to amplify as the silence stretched. Finally, the latch clicked, and the door creaked open to reveal her. Her eyes, red-rimmed and swollen, betrayed a recent storm of tears, and the surrounding skin was puffy.

"You shouldn't have left," he whispered. His hand reached up to cup her cheek. "I wanted to wake up next to you."

"No," she said, shoving his hand away.

He frowned, his brow furrowing, and swiftly pulled his hand back.

"Don't do that," he murmured, stepping forward, but her hand stopped him.

"You're not coming in," she mumbled. He could see the tears welling in her eyes, reflecting the dim light like tiny, shimmering stars. He heard the faint tremor in her voice as she spoke.

"What do you mean?" His brow furrowed, a deep V etched above his nose as his eyes, like slow-moving spotlights, surveyed her, taking in every

detail. A silent assessment, punctuated only by the soft rustle of his clothing. *Last night she was compliant, giving in to whatever it is between us. Now she is crying and acting as if I am a villain.*

"I mean, I can't do this."

"This?"

"Whatever this thing between us is, I'm done. I want you to leave and never come back."

His gaze softened, pupils widening slightly as he murmured, "That whatever thing is something special if you quit fighting it." The words tasted like ash in his mouth, heavy with the emotions threatening to spill over, and he focused on keeping his voice steady, a calm island in the storm raging within.

"No, it's not," she grumbled, her voice throaty and hoarse. Anger flashed across her face, mixing with the sadness swirling in those eyes. "I've been around a lot longer than you and know this is nothing special. You're young and don't yet understand much about life, but you will one day."

The icy sting of her words echoed in his chest, a physical heartbreak that made him reel. He longed to lash out, to argue, to deny the truth that hung heavy in the air like a funeral shroud, but the rawness of his emotions was a stinging wound. Instead, those raw, wounded feelings retreated, shrinking into the shadows of his heart, a dark, silent retreat from the harsh glare of reality. He inhaled deeply, the air thick with unspoken words, straightened his shoulders, and offered a curt nod, a silent acknowledgment.

"Come on, Harlow," he murmured while a smirk across his face to hide his true feelings. "That's a cop-out. I'll leave for now, but we both know you don't want me to go." His voice, a low hum, vibrated in the air as

he stepped back. His smile spread wider, a flash of white as he watched her anger vanish like smoke. For a heartbeat, a moment of softness glazed her hazel eyes, like sunlight filtering through amber glass. "Don't worry, I'll be back."

Her face scrunched up as she looked at the ground. "Don't," she murmured before shutting the door with a soft thud.

Johnna Dee

Weave Your Dreams, Brew Your Magic in

Rusthollow

Harlow

Chapter 15

Harlow the thud sound was almost deafening to her ears. The tears that had been threatening to spill for the entire conversation finally fell free. Walking down the hallway, Shadow mewed, but she ignored him as she continued to walk. Falling onto the bed, the tears and anguish came roaring out.

Scenes from her past flickered before her eyes: the harsh glare of the sun on cracked pavement, the distant, muffled yells of an angry father, and the metallic tang of fear rising in her throat. Her memories, once dormant, now clawed at her, bringing with them the weight of her past. The echo of his mother's sharp words, like shards of glass, cut through her thoughts, each syllable a vivid sting. 'You have been around long enough to know he will grow bored. For your own sake, I suggest you cut him off before you get too invested.'

"Problem is I am already invested," she murmured to herself.

A sob escaped, a small, warm body brushing her leg. She gathered Shadow, a black blur through her tears, into her arms. She inhaled his familiar scent, clinging to his soft fur as he nestled close. His warmth was a meager comfort against the crushing sorrow.

"I should have stayed away from him. Why would I have given in to this... this... whatever this was?"

No answers arose, either from her heart or her mind. She tried to shut the world out, squeezing her eyes shut against the blurry, dark red world behind them, yet the salty tears still flowed, tracing hot paths down her cheeks. Hours of tears later, she fell into a fitful sleep, haunted by the past horrors.

Weave Your Dreams, Brew Your Magic in

Rusthollow

March 13, 1929

Blood, a crimson tear, snaked down nineteen-year-old Harlow's lip, from where her cut had re-opened anew. Her face pulsed with a dull, throbbing ache from Frank Gillespie's brutal blows. The memory of her father's stern voice, demanding her hand in marriage to the older farmer, replayed in her mind every night he raised a fist to her. The farmer was twenty years older than she was, and she had not wanted to marry him, but her father took the choice away from her. Frank's broken promises echoed—to take care of her and give her everything her heart desired—each one a fresh wound as soon as the ink dried on the marriage certificate. Each time she defied or tried to escape this life, she faced a renewed, merciless assault.

The sting of each blow still throbbed on her left side, a symphony of aches. His drunken slurs faded as his heavy breathing became the only sound in the room. A stale smell of alcohol and sweat hung in the air

as he finally passed out.

She crammed the last of her meager possessions into the worn suitcase. She put her best dress on; ironically; it was also her wedding dress. Her gaze fell on her reflection in the scuffed-up mirror. The cream-colored dress had seed pearls glinting in the dim candlelight. It cascaded as it fell below the knee. The drop-waist, with a gentle curve, loosened into a straight fit. The scuffed T-strap heels slipped on easily, the buckles clicking shut. Grabbing the few dollars she had hidden in the flour tin; she stuffed them in her purse. Clutching her suitcase, she slipped out the front door. Outside, the quiet air held the scent of damp earth.

Hope had faded, leaving only the bitter taste of regret. Job hunting had been a harsh lesson: no one wanted her, uneducated and with no experience.

The last of her coins clinked in her palm. Alone, she sat on a cold park bench, the night air chilling her skin. A woman approached, her presence almost glowing. Blonde hair cascaded around a face framed by startling blue eyes, an almost angelic vision.

"Are you hungry?" the angel asked; her smile almost seemed to light up the night. "I know a spot, and I can get you a bite of food."

"Yes," Harlow replied, knowing she had just one more meal left worth of money.

The angel's hand, small and pale against the moonlight, reached out. She took it, the cool metal of a ring brushing her skin. Uncertainty gnawed, but the promise of avoiding spending the last of her money to get food was too much to resist. Pulled forward, the rhythmic thump-thump of her heart echoed the distant city's pulse. They entered a diner; the air was thick with the scent of fried potatoes. She felt her mouth salivate from the wonderful smells. The angel's voice,

a soft murmur, ordered a burger and a strawberry malt. When the waitress brought the food over, the angel slid it in front of her.

"Aren't you going to eat?" Harlow asked her before digging in.

The angel shook her head. "I'm not hungry yet..."

"What's your name?" Harlow took a bite. The burger, a vision of stacked perfection, felt like a gourmet dream against the rough edges of hunger. The first bite, a burst of savory delight. She sipped the malt, the icy sweetness washing over her, a cool balm that filled a hollow ache she hadn't known was there.

"What do you think my name is?" the angel giggled.

"I have no clue," Harlow laughed.

"What's your name?"

"Harlow..." The name hung in the air, a silent question. Should she use her married name, her maiden name, or something else entirely? Her gaze drifted, scanning the room until it landed on a box of chocolates, its glossy paper reflecting the dim light. "Rathmore," she said, reading the name out loud.

Before her mother died, they'd visit town, the vibrant shopfront that sold Rathmore Chocolates beckoning. Inside, she remembered the sweet aroma of cocoa and sugar that hung heavy in the air, like a warm, comforting embrace. They'd sit, the delicate flavors of the treats melting on their tongues, a shared, bittersweet pleasure; the name itself felt like a poignant echo to a happier time.

"Harlow Rathmore," the angel smirked. "Harlow." The name just rolled off her tongue. "My new

friend Lo-lo, it's nice to meet you. I am Ilta Lovelace."

"It's nice to meet you, Ilta." Harlow smiled widely as a chuckle escaped her lips.

After the meal, Ilta invited her to watch Blues Hex, a live jazz band, play at a barn outside of town. They hitched a ride in a beat-up truck and arrived at the old, rundown farmhouse, the music already soaring, filling her ears with a vibrant tune. Her feet tapped to the rhythm as they neared the barn doors. A security guard stood, eyebrow arched, by the entrance.

"Oh yes," Ilta laughed. "The security code." Ilta licked her teeth before speaking. "Blood moon."

The guard swept his arm wide, and they entered. Harlow's eyes scanned the vast room. A kaleidoscope of faces, of every height, color, and style of dress, filled the space. The scent of perfume and sweat hung in the air. Bodies swayed, moved by the singer's husky voice, each note vibrating in her chest.

Her gaze locked onto him. Tall and handsome, with his jet-black hair slicked back, gleaming under the swaying stage light. Those same black eyes seemed to pierce her, though she knew he couldn't see her.

Ilta elbowed her, laughing. "That's Joe Dean Razer or better known as Razor Tongue. His voice is so smooth it just slides all the clothes off a girl like a razor blade."

"You sound like you know this from experience," Harlow giggled.

Ilta, with a playful roll of her eyes, tugged her onto the dance floor. The upbeat jazz pulsed, a vibrant sound that vibrated through her feet. They swung into the lindy hop, the music's rhythm a physical thing. They danced and drank, Harlow blissfully unaware of

her worries. The potent alcohol burned on the way down as she enjoyed the illegal substance. Suddenly, Ilta was gone. Harlow looked around the packed room, then stumbled toward the barn door. The music stopped playing, but the crowd's voices still filled the space. The rough wood was cool beneath her fingertips as she pushed, but it wouldn't budge.

"Well, ain't you a pretty lil thang," the smooth voice she had been listening to all night said from behind her.

She turned, meeting those midnight eyes, dark pools reflecting nothing. A chill snaked up her spine, a prickle of unease raising gooseflesh on her arms. The sudden urge to flee slammed into her, a frantic pounding in her chest. She just knew, with a certainty that echoed in the sudden silence, that she needed to listen.

"Thank you," she murmured, her gaze flitting towards the wooden ladder behind the bar's dim lights. Having grown up on a farm, she knew the familiar climb would offer an escape. The thought of jumping in heels made her stomach clench, but she knew it was the only option she had with the barn door being locked.

She sidestepped Joe Dean, but his hand shot out, fingers clamping down on her arm, the sharp pressure a jolt of pain. Her gaze snapped up to his face, and the reason for her sudden urge to flee crystallized in that moment. *It's the look in his eyes. That's the same look Frank would get before he beat me.*

She smiled at him sweetly. "I just want to go get another shot, and then maybe we can hang out."

"Alright," he smirked.

He turned back to his bandmates, the chatter of the crowd a dull roar around them. The bassist's words,

a low rumble, hinted at something delicious, but she saw no food. Her eyes flitted to the band as she moved into the bar's dimness. The wooden ladder felt rough under her hands as she ascended, the weak light barely reaching her. Initially, the bustling crowd was oblivious. Then, nearing the next floor, a scream pierced the air. Spinning, she saw the double bass player, teeth sunk into a dancer's shoulder. Fear surged, propelling her up the ladder. Her feet pounded the wooden floor as she ran across the loft. The hayloft door loomed, and she flung it open.

"Lo-lo," Razor's voice came from behind her.

How does he know my name? Ilta was in on it, and I fell for her ploy,

She turned, his approach a blur of red, blood slicking his face. Without pause, she leapt. Her legs buckled on impact, a sharp sting lancing her ankle. Across the lawn, she ran, each step a lurch. She knew that miles away was any house that might offer help, but the darkened farmhouse loomed in front of her. A phone, keys, a weapon: safety was her only thought. Before the door, his grip seized her waist, teeth plunging into her neck. Gasping, she swung, her elbow connecting with his ear. He grunted, releasing her. Warm blood trickled down her neck.

She saw the glint of the axe beside the weathered porch stairs. Grabbing it, she swung, connecting with a wet thwack against his arm. He bellowed out a roar. Turning, she bolted into the shadowed house, the lock clicking shut behind her. Fear, cold and sharp, twisted her gut. The musty air of the rundown house swirled as she clutched her shoulder, feeling the sticky warmth of blood. Her grey dress was now soaked crimson. Heavy footsteps thudded closer. Her heart hammered a frantic rhythm, threatening to burst. Her head swam, vision narrowing with black spots.

She stumbled, the roughness of the wall scraping her cheek as she fell. A jarring crack echoed as her body hit. Crimson stained her vision as her bloodied hands smeared the walls, a chilling trail in the dim hall.

"Lo-lo," a menacing voice said in a singsong tone. "Do you really think you can run from me?"

The thud of approaching footsteps echoed, each one a hammer against her racing heart. She lurched into the kitchen, grabbing the first drawer she saw and tugging. She yanked open drawer after drawer, a frantic clatter filling the air as her vision swam.

"There you are, Lo-lo," he whispered.

Her hands, clammy with sweat, latched onto the rough surface. She gripped the cool wooden handle, its texture a stark contrast to her heated skin, and concealed it behind her back. He spun her, a dizzying rush of motion, his dark eyes gleaming with manic glee, fixed on her.

"While it has been so much fun playing cat and mouse, the sun is coming up soon and I need to feed," he growled.

His teeth pierced her shoulder, a searing pain exploding outward as he drank. The metallic tang of blood filled the air. She brandished the cold steel of the kitchen knife, the dull glint reflecting the harsh light, and plunged it into his chest, his back and his head, in a desperate rhythm that had no aim. He staggered and then crashed to the floor. Fury consumed her as she fell upon him, her hand a relentless piston. His blood sprayed, a wet, coppery taste invading her mouth and her wounds as she kept swinging. Tears streamed down her face as she pulled away, a fresh, agonizing pain blooming through her whole body.

She awoke with a jolt, the sudden movement

sending a prickle of unease across her skin. The echo of the promise she made, a vow etched deep within her memory all those years ago, resonated in the quiet air. *I once trusted the wrong person, and that had left me broken. I will let no one have the power to break me again.*

Aris

Chapter 16

Aris paced his room. Since leaving Harlow's house, a hollow ache resonated with each footfall on the cold marble floor. He tried to mask the turmoil, but the worried glances of his parents pricked like needles. His heart throbbed, and his thoughts swirled like dust devils. He wanted to drive back over and force her to see what was right in front of her. He wanted to escape, to soothe his wounded soul. Instead, he stomped around the house like a caged lion.

Unable to sleep, he yanked the curtains. Sunlight, a searing white flash that kissed his skin, was a fiery touch that made him recoil with a bellow. Blackout curtains slammed shut, but his arm still bore angry red scorch marks. The thunder of approaching footsteps echoed as he stared at the damaged skin, fear a cold knot in his stomach.

"Aris!" his mom shrieked as the door flew open. "Ooh, my baby!"

She dashed towards him, her own hands trembling as they hovered over his wounded arm. "Let me call a healer." Amara's sandals thudded as she ran off.

"What the hell were you thinking, boy?" Tiberias growled.

"I forgot for a moment," Aris huffed.

"This is something you can't forget." Tiberias shook his head, the words hanging heavy in the air. "Things are different now, and you have been trained for this situation. You should know better."

Amara dashed back into the room. "Okay. The healer is on their way. Arca should be here soon. Oh, my sweet Lambkin, what were you thinking?"

"Obviously, I wasn't thinking." Aris sighed, the sound heavy in the close air, a blush creeping up his neck. He felt like an idiot.

"My love, you need to be careful now." Amara exhaled heavily. "I know you are used to the sun, but things like this can scar you for life or worse. The sun is no longer your friend. I will have shutters over your windows installed so this can't happen again." Her hand, cool against his skin, rose and cupped his cheek. "I can't stand to watch you hurting, so can you please be more careful, lambkin?"

"Yes, Mom," he murmured, feeling like a little boy being lectured.

Amara glanced over her shoulder, her brow furrowed. Her worried gaze met Tiberias. "We will have to be extra vigilant until he gets used to this."

Tiberias nodded, his face a mask of shadows as he stepped back into the hallway, the gesture heavy with unspoken words.

"I don't need a babysitter," Aris grumbled, rolling his eyes. "I fucked up once; lesson learned. This won't happen again. Can we change the subject?"

Tiberias's lips curled into a smirk as he shook his head.

"Are you sassing me?" Amara swatted his chest.

"No." Aris whispered, his voice a tight sound. He swiveled, his gaze locking onto his dad, and the desperation in his wide eyes was palpable.

Tiberias's eyes grew wide as he shook his head again.

"Come downstairs if you're not in too much pain," Amara huffed, putting her hand on the small of his back and guiding him towards the door. "I mean, you have to be in serious amounts of pain to use that sassy mouth of yours at a time like this."

Aris groaned, the sound echoing in the stuffy stairwell, as he trailed his mother. Each step jarred, sending a fresh throb through his arm. The air hung thick, faintly metallic, and the burning of his wound was now a dull, more tolerable ache.

Within twenty minutes, Arca Thornheart arrived, the owner of the Arca Apothecary. Her brassy red hair escaped its messy bun, catching the light and shimmering. Her chocolate-brown eyes, a blend of weariness and cheer, sparkled.

"Let me see the wound," she murmured.

The cool, slick ointment spread across his skin, followed by the bandage. A sharp "tsk" sound punctuated each movement.

He could feel the salve starting to work as the throb turned to ache and then vanished altogether. His mind swirled as his mother left the room with Arca.

"Boy, I'll only say it once more, be careful." Tiberias gently patted Aris on the back.

Looking up, the angles of his face, almost a mirror of his own, struck him. He inhaled, the coppery tang of blood filling his nostrils. A familiar scent, yet elusive in its memory, clung to the air.

"Why won't you tell me where I came from?" the words slipped past his lips before he could even pro-

cess his emotions.

"Some things are best left unknown." Tiberias's brow furrowed as a deep frown spread across his lips.

"Maybe some secrets are best told instead of shoved in some dark corner for all eternity."

Standing, he let out a heavy sigh as he stepped out. The door clicked shut. He wasn't sure why the truth still beckoned, yet it did. The phantom need to know was a cold wave crashing over him, always present, a lingering shadow in the background of his mind. *My emotions are just raw because of Harlow. Maybe it's best I don't ask anymore. Obviously, no one will ever tell me the truth.*

As twilight bled into night, Aris wrestled with the decision: give Harlow space or push again? Impatience gnawed at him. His thoughts, a chaotic storm, crashed over him. He felt the sting of Harlow's resistance against what he knew she desired. He saw red, fueled by the secrecy of his past. An icy dread settled as helplessness washed over him. *I hate that no one seems to want to talk to me about what is important. Only what they want to hear themselves.*

The clock's chime sliced through the quiet, a jarring sound that sparked a wash of relief and frustration within him. The cold plastic of the clock, a recent addition to his bedroom, sat heavy on his nightstand, a constant reminder of when it was alright to go outside.

Somehow, Mom always finds a way to make me feel like a little boy still.

With a bound, he was airborne, flying down the stairs as they creaked under the weight of his descent.

"Where are you going, my boy?" From the stairwell's shadowed height, Tiberias's voice echoed. Aris paused at the bottom of the stairs.

Aris turned to look at his father. "Nowhere special, just drive around. You know, get out and grab some air."

Before his dad could respond, he bolted to the kitchen and left. The engine roared, a guttural growl echoing as he sped down the driveway. He dropped the top, the icy air a shock, swirling around him. Anger fueled the gas pedal as he took curves, wind whipping his hair. Some frustration blew away in the cool breeze as the car whipped around the curves with ease.

Pulling into a parking spot, eyes darted, seeing her little truck parked. He walked the short distance to the apartment. He knocked, the sound echoing in the quiet. Minutes passed before the door creaked open. A faint lilac perfume—her scent—wafted towards him. With his newfound vampire senses heightened; he heard her calm, steady heartbeat. A smaller, quicker beat accompanied it.

"Umm, hi," she mumbled.

"I said I'd be back." A slow smile spread across his face as he leaned against the wooden doorjamb. His gaze, dark and intense, traveled up and down her, a silent, assessing survey. Harlow stood in soft, worn sweatpants and a baggy shirt, the cotton clinging lightly to her curves. *That is weirdly hot.*

"That you did." His gaze followed her as she ran

her hands over the soft, gray fabric of her sweatpants, a gesture that appeared self-conscious. "I could have sworn I told you not to."

His hand, cool and smooth, snaked up, grazing her warm neck. A soft rush filled his ears as her heartbeat quickened, a rapid drum against the quiet. "We both know that was a lie when you said it then as it is now. I can hear that little heart speed up at my touch."

"That's just from..." she paused, her eyes squinting. "Annoyance."

Shaking his head, he said, "I wish you'd stop lying; it's unattractive."

"Not enough for you to leave me alone."

His hand curved around the smooth, cool skin at the back of her neck. "So, you admit you know you're lying?"

"Wait, what?" she inhaled.

Laughing, he leaned in closer to her. "Why are you fighting?"

"We should talk about the other night," she started. "It was—"

"Something we should recreate," he interrupted. He stepped forward, the floorboards groaning under his weight, prompting her to step back. The heavy door shut with a resounding thud, trapping them in near darkness. His eyes adjusted to the dim light. Her rapid heartbeat echoed in his ears, a frantic rhythm.

"No," she said, putting her hand on his chest. "It was a one-off mistake, and it won't happen again."

A snorting laugh left his mouth. "I can prove you wrong."

She shook her head, the movement a blur against the dim light. When he pulled her close, her fist knotted in his shirt, but she offered no fight as she was drawn against his chest. His mouth crashed down, a forceful assault met with the sweet yielding taste of her as his tongue swept in. Her body surrendered, soft and pliant against his hard form. His hand found her, cupping her ass and lifting her; her legs wrapped around his waist, a tight, squeezing embrace.

Turning, he pinned her to the wall. The scent of her perfume and blood filled his nostrils. He pressed his shaft hard into her yielding flesh, the pressure intense. A low groan rumbled from his chest.

He pulled his mouth a breath away. "I was going to be polite, but your lips are making it really hard to stay well-behaved."

Harlow

Chapter 17

Harlow glared, wanting to fight, knowing it was the best option. But the second he touched her, all thoughts vanished. A rush of only feelings he could make her feel exploded within her. His fingers, drumsticks, drummed a rhythm her heart echoed as they kneaded her ass.

His rigid shaft pressed against her yielding flesh. She felt the building heat in her core despite the turmoil in her mind. No matter how much her mind raged, her body always gave in to his touch. His lips found hers once more, a demanding pressure as she parted for him. A soft moan escaped, and she surrendered to the kiss.

A hand shot up, fingers tangling in her bun, yanking her head back. The world tilted. A low growl rumbled, and then, the faintest rasp of his fangs, a whisper of cold against the vulnerable skin of her neck.

The soft rasp of his inhale preceded the slick slide of his tongue across her throat. His warm breath danced over the damp path he'd created. "Your body," he murmured, his voice a low rumble, "is saying things your lips won't—yet"

The words hung in the air, sharp and unwelcome. She wanted to deny them, to battle the visions they conjured within her, but the fight had drained away, leaving only the need for him.

His rough hands pressed harder against

her yielding flesh, the tips of his fingers digging into the soft curve of her ass, pressing her closer. The wind whooshed in her lungs as his fangs sank into her throat, a sharp, stinging pain blooming. The coppery tang of blood mixed with the earthy scent of his skin as pleasure and pain radiated from the tiny punctures. Her fingers tangled in the silky strands of his hair. He retracted his fangs, his tongue a warm rasp against her neck as he licked the wounds while they healed.

"You taste mouthwatering, my little delicacy," he murmured, his nose brushing her ear.

He shoved her legs off his waist. His rugged hands turned her. The cool, textured wall met her front. His hands traveled, finding her waistband. With a firm tug, the fabric whispered as it fell. His hands roamed, causing a breathless gasp. He pressed against her back, the denim of his jeans a coarse contrast to her skin. His hand moved lower, finding her core. His fingers, light as a whisper, traced her moist lips. A moan escaped as her head tilted back onto his shoulder.

"Want more?" His tongue flicked her earlobe.

She bit her tongue, the sharp sting a sudden jolt as her fangs pierced flesh. A coppery tang bloomed in her mouth.

His calloused hands stilled their soft ministrations. A hushed voice, like a dry leaf skittering across stone, whispered, "Answer my question, little delicacy."

"Yes," she growled, craving more.

Two fingers slid inside her, the slickness a cool contrast to the heat building within. Her hips bucked, meeting his thrusts, the pressure intensifying. A sharp intake of breath, the scrape of teeth on skin, a nibble on her shoulder. Inside, the rhythm quickened. Each thrust of his fingers sent a shiver down her spine, every

nerve ending alight with pleasure. Then, the sudden absence—his fingers, his touch, his presence—vanished.

She pivoted, but a hand, heavy, pinned her back. A whisper of fabric rustled behind her. Her gaze flickered over her shoulder, capturing the sight of his skin as clothes peeled away, revealing sculpted muscles. Her eyes lingered, tracing the curve of his body from his feet, pausing at his thick shaft, before climbing to his forest green eyes, now dark with desire. A slow smile played on his lips before he moved closer.

She felt his hard, stiff member press against her butt. One hand kneaded her breast; she felt the heat of his palm, while the other strummed her clit. His fangs scraped her earlobe, a rough, thrilling sensation before he sucked it in, a wet pull. Her body bloomed, a blossoming warmth, under his skilled fingers. His hand slid down her torso, meeting the other at her core. Then, two fingers entered her, while the other hand circled her clit. Her hips pressed against his hand, then back, feeling his hard shaft on her backside. She heard him groan, a low growl, his teeth sinking into her earlobe, causing her to move again. Feeling bolder, she pressed harder against his stiffness. Pressing against him again, her skin brushed his, a forceful friction as his growing hardness pressed back. He pressed her hard against the wall as his fingers continued to play her like a guitar.

Her trembling hands were balled into fists against the cold, rough wall. His mouth, a wet heat, moved from her ear to her neck. She felt the sharp scrape of his fangs as he suckled. His other hand circled, fingers plunging, her core clenching with each thrust. Ragged breaths escaped her, her legs quivering.

His hand left her clit, and a frustrated growl escaped her lips. She craved more of his touch, of him. His firm hand traced down her inner thigh before

clutching and lifting her leg up. His palm pressed her bent knee against the wall. A swift thrust filled her, eliciting a gasp. Each thrust made her clench tighter. His grip on her thigh got tighter as the fingers dug into it while the other hand strummed her clit faster. She could feel herself spiraling into oblivion with each touch, each thrust, and each circle on her bundle of nerves. His chest, a rock against her back, pinned her. Her hand found his on her thigh, clinging. Harsh, fast breaths filled the air. His breath fluttered against her hair, then teeth bit her shoulder as she climaxed. The release rocked her.

If he hadn't held her, she'd have crumpled, hitting the cold floor. The racing in her chest gradually calmed, each breath less ragged. The lingering heat of passion dissipated, replaced by a flood of worried thoughts. Self-doubt and fear filled her, gripped her heart with all the overwhelming emotions that had clawed at her for months.

"We can't do this again," she whispered, feeling her own heart breaking at the sound of her own voice.

"Why do you keep doing that?" he said, kissing her neck. His nose nuzzled her ear, sending a shiver down her spine.

"You are young and don't understand," she whispered, trying to hide the tears pricking her eyes.

"Not too young to know what I want in life." His hand released her thigh, letting it slide down the wall.

"What you want, but you never ask what I want." Her gaze, sharp as broken glass, fixed on him over her shoulder. The urge to grab his hand, to feel his touch against her skin, burned like a fever—she craved his touch as much as she craved the blood that sustained her life. But she remained still, a statue against the cold, unforgiving wall.

"I know you want me," he growled, pushing away. "I can see it in your eyes, hear it in your heartbeat."

"Lust is easy. It comes and goes." The phrase hung heavy in the air. She faced the cold blue walls; a paint color she spent so much time on that once brought her joy now made her stomach churn. The silence amplified the pounding of her heart, too terrified to meet his gaze and reveal the truth.

"What?"

"This is just lust. It'll vanish soon, so we might as well stop this before things turn sour, like they will eventually." A sharp intake of breath, a visible tremor in her posture, and her face hardened, the softness of her features replaced by a stoic mask. "There is nothing else I want from you. I don't want to date you. I don't want to talk to you. All I want is for you to leave me alone."

"You don't mean that." His voice, a shaky tremor, resonated with a depth of feeling that resonated with a conviction that almost broke her.

"That's the thing," she murmured, her voice a low hum. Her footsteps whispered on the floor as she moved, grabbing his clothes from the floor, the air still and carrying the scent of their passion. With a quick flick of her wrist, she sent his clothes tumbling through the air, landing with a soft thud against his chest. "This was fun, but that's all it was. I am not interested in flirting with you or anything else."

"You know, I'm actually pretty terrible at flirting now that you mention it," he murmured, staring off into the distance.

"Agreed," she snorted with a harsh laugh. "Maybe you should stop."

"You're right," he shrugged. "Maybe I should, since I am just a boy, and how could I possibly understand. How about when you pull whatever stick that's shoved up there out of your ass and you realize we could be something you can try to pick me up instead?"

"Never going to happen. This was a mistake, and it will never, *never* happen again."

Johnna Dee

Aris

Chapter 18

$\mathbf{A}$ris sat on the porch, the pre-dawn chill prickling his skin as he waited. From the looks of the moon, he still had three hours until sunrise. His gaze traced the long, empty driveway. He'd hoped for Harlow, but the silence confirmed she wouldn't come. The last vestiges of hope vanished as he sipped the crimson liquid his father had given him, the metallic tang coating his tongue. He remembered her taste, a sweetness now soured by her words. He slammed his fist on the chair's worn arm, the wood groaning, then rose and went inside.

I must be an idiot. Waiting for a woman who has told me multiple times she isn't interested. Maybe I should have listened to her from the start and not my heart.

He slammed his bedroom door. The loud thud vibrated through the floorboards, failing to quell his anger. A soft knock resounded, drawing his gaze. His ears strained, picking up the rhythmic thump on the other side—a heartbeat. Concentrating, he recognized his mother's familiar cadence. The more he listened, the more he noticed the unique rhythm of everyone's heartbeat.

"What?" he said. His voice, thick with unspoken anger, even though he tried to hide it.

"Can I come in?" Amara barely whispered the words; a faint breath of sound almost lost in the air. Only his enhanced hearing, a newly awakened sense, allowed him to catch the sound.

"Sure," he sighed, the sound a soft exhale in the quiet room. He felt the familiar give of the mattress as he plopped down on the edge of the bed.

"What's going on, lambkin?" she murmured. She walked over to him, the rustle of her skirt a soft whisper. Reaching him, her fingers, cool against his skin, smoothed his hair down.

"Nothing," he shrugged.

"Don't brush me off like that." Amara shook her head.

"I'm just in a mood. Don't worry about it. So, go back to whatever it was you were doing and leave me alone."

"Aris Tiberias Damascus," she said in a stern tone. "You will not dismiss me like that. You will answer me, instead of sulking around the house, slamming doors left and right."

"It was one door."

"No, two. The front door and your bedroom door. Then add in your stomping up the stairs like a herd of elephants."

"Don't be dramatic," he huffed.

Amara's gaze locked onto him, a stormy look in her blue eyes. The rhythmic tap-tap of her foot against the floor filled the otherwise silent room. She crossed her arms across her chest, then spoke, "Just because you are in a bad mood doesn't mean you can talk to me like that."

"I am not talking like anything. I just don't feel like talking right now."

"Then end the conversation faster by telling me what's bothering you."

"If I tell you, will you leave me to my misery?"

"Yes," she whispered.

He knew she wouldn't leave him alone, but part of him wondered if in speaking the words, in getting it off his chest, it would make him feel better. "Fine."

Amara settled on the bed, her head a weight on his shoulder. Her arm slid into his, fingers interlacing. He gazed at his mom's tiny, pale hand nestled in his. "I'm all ears."

Exhaling, he grumbled, "I thought Harlow felt the same about me as I did for her, and apparently I was wrong."

He felt Amara stiffen beside him, the subtle tension against his arm. "What do you mean?" she queried.

"She doesn't give a shit about me," he heaved out. "That should make you happy. So, you can show me all the fang bangers you want. I don't care anymore."

"Are you truly miserable?" Amara asked, her voice twinged with a note of sadness.

His ears twitched, catching the rapid thump of her heart. A crease formed between his brows.

"Nothing time won't heal." His hand, large and clumsy, landed on her knee with a soft thud. The gesture felt stiff, a clumsy dance of awkward comfort. "Go arrange whatever political alliance you want. Just make sure she isn't annoying."

Amara rose. Aris saw the dullness in her downcast eyes before her shoulders slumped and she turned,

the rustle of her skirt fading as she departed.

Sinking onto the bed, he sank into the yielding mattress, gazing at the white ceiling. A chaotic jumble of thoughts swirled in his mind. He rubbed his eyes with rough palms, attempting to erase the mental clutter, but it stubbornly remained.

The rhythmic thump echoed, a hushed drumbeat in his ears. Then, the door slammed wide. *Why can't I have a moment of peace in this big old house, for fuck's sake?*

"What do you want, Dad?" he grunted, sitting back up.

"Woman troubles?" Tiberias asked with a smirk.

"I don't need or want advice from you, old man."

"How about an ear to listen to?" Tiberias patted him on the back. "I have had woman troubles, you know that, right? I have been—"

"You've been married for over a hundred and fifty years. I highly doubt you can relate," he huffed.

"Boy," Tiberias growled. "Your mother just drove out of here like a bat out of hell. Don't think I don't know it has something to do with what's bothering you. Just because I have been married for a hundred and forty-eight years, to be exact, doesn't mean I know nothing about women, single or married. So don't give me lip."

"Maybe it's hard to want to talk to someone who has always kept major secrets from me." The words tumbled out, sharp and unexpected, hanging in the air like shattered glass. He didn't know why he'd spoken to them or why he'd pressed the button, he knew it would anger his dad, but he felt a burning need to inflict pain,

a matching ache to his own.

"Why do we have to circle around this topic again and again?" Tiberias groaned.

"Maybe because my whole life I've felt this part of me was missing," Aris growled, the words a low rumble. He jumped up; the sudden movement was a blur and paced. His earlier sadness evaporated, replaced by a simmering anger that prickled across his skin. "And you guys hold that piece locked away so I can never get it back. Instead of being honest with me and letting me see it, you get defensive and angry or crack some kind of sarcastic joke."

"Maybe because I am keeping you safe, boy!" Tiberias yelled back.

"From what?" Aris threw his hands in the air. "Is someone going to murder me if I know the truth? Will I perpetually be nothing more than a *boy* to you? If that's the case, then there's no point in this conversation about my sex life."

"When you act like a man, I'll treat you like one," Tiberias screamed. The emerald of his eyes blazed, a scorching inferno, mirroring the heat that flushed his skin.

The cold fury crystallized across his skin, a chilling presence. His words, though level, were edged with the rasp of steel. "Alright. I'll leave and prove I can be a man on my own."

Tiberias exhaled, a long, rasping sound that seemed to fill the silent room. His gaze traveled upward, finally settling on the ceiling. Then his eyes locked back with Aris's. "I'm sorry, Aris. I have spent years trying to be a good father. Can we start over with this conversation? It went off the rails."

"Maybe I don't want to start over," Aris growled. "Maybe I just want honesty from the people around me instead of being pushed away or told how they're keeping me safe."

"I was trying to protect you from getting hurt."

The words—thick and suffocating—lingered in the silent room. Aris's jaw clenched, the heat of anger fading, replaced by a hollow chill that settled in his chest. "They hated me that much?"

"No," Tiberias huffed as he sat on the edge of the bed. "Are you sure you want to know?"

"Yes."

Tiberias patted the spot next to him on the bed. "Sit, please."

Aris sank onto the bed. He closed his eyes, the dim light of the room flickering behind his eyelids. He inhaled sharply, focusing on each breath, a technique his father, with his calloused hands and deep voice, had drilled into him long ago. *You can't control what you feel, but you can control your breathing.*

"A hundred and fifty years ago, before I met Amara and was turned, I was married to a human. I had a human life. Including having a child. My first wife died during childbirth." Tiberias paused, taking a few deep breaths.

"What does this have to do with anything now, and why did you never tell me about this before?" Aris whispered.

"I'm getting there," Tiberias laughed, a self-deprecating sound. The corners of his eyes crinkled as he spoke, and he shifted slightly. "Just be patient. The marriage was an arranged marriage, so when she died,

her parents wanted to raise the baby without me. They said a single male could not raise a child alone. At first, I fought them, not wanting to give up my son. Then I met Amara, and everything changed. I knew I was going to be turned and didn't think I could raise a toddler after being newly turned, so I gave the kid to his grandparents. They were good people, and I knew they would do right by him."

A tense silence hung in the air, thick enough to taste, as Aris sought the connection to himself. He'd never truly considered his father's life before being turned, or his mother for that matter. They'd always just been as they are now in his mind. He focused on his father, trying to see the human he once was.

"The times were tough," Tiberias continued. "Not just in the human world, but in the vampire world. There was a struggle in our coven, a fight to figure out who would lead us. As I fought for control, I had watched from a distance throughout the years as the boy, Lucius, grew. I never let him see me again or tried to turn them. I kept tabs on his kids and their kids throughout the years. It was just a marvel to see them and how their lives grew and changed. Then Cyris was born. Even from a young age, she was just so ornery, different. When she was a teen, she started dabbling in drugs. Addiction quickly followed. Next thing we knew, she was pregnant. She told no one who the birth father was. She seemed to shape up, to stop doing drugs. A beautiful baby boy was born. Then I got word she was back on drugs. At one month old, she had left the baby alone for an entire day. No food, no nothing. Just this innocent little creature alone. I went to check on you. Who knows how long you had been crying there. You were just one month old, and she had left you alone. Amara took one look at you, and I remember vividly her words. He is ours, and we can't just leave him here. She just accepted you and loved you from the second she saw you. She just picked you up and cradled you.

Like magic, you stopped fussing."

Tiberias paused, as if lost in thought for a brief moment. "I found her at an Elysian Essence Den. She was so high she just lost track of time."

Aris had never tried Elysian Essence. It's a sweet, pastel-hued tablet that whispers promises of serenity, but leads you down a rabbit hole of paranoia, fear, and addiction.

"It didn't take long to negotiate with her in exchange for you. We knew the instant we took you in that in our world we could not keep your human forever. But we could not just hand you back to her. It was then we announced the decision to have you turn on your twenty-first birthday." Tiberias rested his elbows on his knees, his shoulders sagging.

He absorbed his father's words as the silence seemed to stretch out. A kaleidoscope of different fantasies had filled his dreams and nightmares as a kid; each one had been a desperate attempt to fill the void left by not knowing who his birth parents were, but he had never had this as a scenario.

"This explains why we look similar," Aris finally broke the silence.

"Is that all you have to say?" Tiberias snorted.

"Would you rather I asked how much my life was worth?"

"No, not really," Tiberias laughed, a quick sound that faded fast. "Just know that whether it was one dollar or a million, I would have paid it. Are you upset?"

"No," Aris shook his head. "Maybe just sad knowing the truth and confused why you thought you couldn't just be honest."

"I never wanted you to feel you didn't belong," Tiberias sighed. "To make sure you never thought that you were unloved because we paid for you. All we ever wanted was to give you a better life."

"Thank you for telling me the truth."

Tiberias nodded. He wrapped his arms around Aris, the familiar weight and warmth a comforting embrace. "I love you, my boy. Man, whatever the hell you want to be called."

Laughing, Aris pushed him away. "Why can't we just call me by my name?"

"Nah," Tiberias laughed, his hand grabbed Aris's head and rubbed his knuckles, a rough, scratchy sensation, on it. "You'll always be my boy. Today, tomorrow, and even a hundred years from now."

Harlow

Chapter 19

Harlow pressed her face into the pillow, the cotton rough against her cheek as warm tears flowed. An hour had passed since his departure, yet his cologne still clung to her skin. Even the hot water hadn't washed it away. A sharp, mournful mew pierced the silence. She jolted, panic gripping her. Racing to the living room, she saw the carnage. The couch arm was a mess of ripped fabric, and fur danced in the air as Shadow's change began. Reaching out, she felt the small body as the sickening cracks and pops of bones reconfiguring filled the room.

"No! No! No!" Harlow scowled. "Not right now, please!"

The insistent mewing pierced the air, escalating with each failed attempt to grasp the slick kitty as it wriggled. Limbs elongated, gaining strength. Coarse fur sprouted, and teeth lengthened, transforming.

"Please stop moving so I can get you in your cage," Harlow growled.

Shadow writhed, the air thick with the stench of ozone, and a guttural howl ripped through the silence. Muscles bulged, bones cracked, and then stillness. Glowing eyes pierced the dimness, locking onto her.

"Fuck," she grumbled. "Don't get us kicked out of another complex. Please be qui-et."

"Shadow," she spoke softly. She crouched, the rough ground pressing against her knees, striving to shrink her form as she met his gaze, the air thick with unspoken tension. "Please come here."

A guttural yowl ripped through the air, originating from her werekitty. The creature, fur bristling, his muscles bulging, had doubled in size after the shift.

"I am so sorry I was lost in my own feelings and forgot it was a full moon," she murmured, trying to use her most soothing voice.

Glowing tawny eyes, like embers, warily watched her as they circled. She pivoted, mirroring his movements, never losing sight of Shadow. He lowered his head, muscles coiled. Anticipating the pounce, she dove, landing with a thud on the wooden floor. Shadow launched for the couch, the daggers at the end of his paws tearing the fabric.

"NO!" she yelped. "I can't afford another couch."

She reached for Shadow again, her fingers stretching. A sharp crack echoed as her knee slammed against the cold, unyielding wood of the coffee table. "Ouch!" she squealed.

Shadow's dark shape blurred, racing down the hall. A rush of adrenaline fueled her dive, the impact sending them both sprawling. The stinging scent of her blood filled the air from his claws as they tore into her arm. She felt his warm, struggling form beneath her while she held him tightly to keep him from escaping.

"You will not get away and destroy anything else, you little bugger," she growled as his teeth sunk into her hand. "Dammit, that hurts!"

With every strained muscle, she dragged him to the cold, steel box that loomed in the living room's corner, destined for his full moon transformations.

She forced him in, each shove adding stinging cuts to her arm. Clang! The heavy door shut, its lock clicking, enclosing him in the four-by-four-foot space. Sliding down the metal, she heard his enraged yowls through the tiny ventilation holes.

Tears, hot and stinging, blurred her vision as she exhaled. Her gaze swept the living room: the once plush sofa sagged, its fabric ripped and springs sticking out, a lost cause. The rug was shredded, lying in tatters. Deep claw marks marred the walls, a testament to the chaos, and the hallway floor bore ugly, gouged scars.

"Can't I just be miserable in peace?" She mumbled as a soft knock on her door rang through the air. "Apparently not."

She pushed up, eyes tracing her arms. Healed cuts and bite marks marred her skin, though her own blood, a sharp crimson, still stained her flesh. The persistent knock echoed again, a steady thump.

"One minute," she responded, running to the kitchen to clean her arms off.

Looking down, she realized Shadow had torn her clothes to shreds. "Ugh. I can't win today, can I?"

Running down the hall, she slammed the closet door open. The scent of cedar and fabric wafted as she tossed aside her shirt and pants. Her fingers closed on cotton, a faded sundress's worn fabric cool against her skin.

The knock came louder this time.

"One minute, please," she screamed.

Calmly walking to the door, she whispered to herself. "Please don't be the landlord. Please don't be the landlord. Please don't be the landlord."

Opening the door a crack. The startling vision in front of her made her pause. "What are you doing here?"

"Are you always so rude to guests? You should invite me in,"

Turning, she surveyed the chaotic house. The howl from the metal box filled the air, a sound that prickled her skin. This, she decided, was a terrible idea. "How about I come outside? It is such a pleasant night."

She stepped out, the cold air nipping at her skin beneath her flimsy dress. A mournful howl echoed from within her house. She debated which was worse, freezing to death or having someone see the nightmare that was her house right now. Harlow plastered on a bright smile, praying to avoid unwanted questions.

"What is that?" Startled eyes met Harlow's.

"How about we take a walk?" Harlow smiled brighter while her eyes pleaded.

"No, you're going to explain what that noise was."

Rolling her eyes, Harlow sighed. "It's my were-kitty. He... ummm... he transforms on a full moon and can get rowdy. What can I help you with tonight?"

"Oh, interesting," Amara murmured. She looked up and down Harlow, soft blue eyes meeting hers. "I can admit when I'm wrong and apologize for it. It's hard to admit it; I won't lie."

Dumbfounded, Harlow stared, the inky blackness of night pressing in. A shiver traced her spine as the night's chill seeped into her skin. The rustle of unseen leaves flowing on the breeze broke the silence only. She rubbed her arms, seeking warmth.

"This is absurd," Amara rolled her eyes. "You are obviously freezing in that," she flicked her wrist, "dress. Let's go inside. I can handle a little werekitty. I've dealt with much worse."

"Umm, well," Harlow stuttered. "He's locked up, but I am fine. Please, just say your piece."

"Are you really going to be that stubborn and not invite me in after I practically apologized?" Amara said, raising a blonde eyebrow.

Harlow stared at Amara, her mind a whirlwind of thoughts. *She has had nothing but a poor opinion of me, so seeing the chaos of my apartment won't matter at this point. It's warmer inside, so at least I will be comfortable while I hear whatever she has to say. Plus, what exactly is she apologizing for?* Feeling the weight of the last few days weighing on her, she shrugged, giving up on hiding the destruction Shadow had created.

Opening the door wide, she gestured Amata in. Her mouth was a tight line.

"Oh," Amara paused in the doorway. "This is quite... charming."

"Thanks for lying," Harlow said, closing the door with a thud.

"You're welcome," Amara sighed. "Is this the werekitty?" Amara walked over to the metal box and tried to peek through one hole. Shadow let out a yowling growl.

"Yes, his name is Shadow. Did you come here to meet him?"

"No, just intrigued." Turning, Amara looked at Harlow. "I guess since you want to get down to business. I apologize for insinuating you were not good

enough for Aris."

"Insinuating?" Harlow snorted.

"You're not going to make this easy, are you?" Amara said, tapping a foot. "Fine. I stated it. As a mother, you make certain," she paused as if searching for words. "Sacrifices for your child, hoping they will have a better life. Choose a better path than you chose. In pushing you away, I was trying to guide him down a path with political alliances that would strengthen our coven. I think you have been alone so long you forget what it's like to consider there is more than just oneself to care for. My son likes you, so I apologize for my cruel words."

Harlow stared uncertainly. The words hit her as she debated how to reply. She decided on simple words. "Apology accepted."

Amara nodded. "But understand one thing: break my son's heart, and I will snap your neck without hesitation. I am powerful enough that no one, and I mean no one, will take a second glance before stepping over your corpse. Do you understand me?"

Harlow noted the way those warm blue eyes turned icy cold with a nod. Harlow finally opened her mouth, speaking, "It won't be a problem since we will not be together."

With a laugh, Amara looked at Shadow's cage. "You'd be a fool to turn him down. He is one of the good ones."

"If you say so."

Harlow stared at the closed door, the wood's smooth surface reflecting the dim light. The ghost of Amara's exit and the distant echo of her own racing thoughts filled her mind. Should she chase after Aris or

clean her apartment? Turning, she sighed, the air thick with the scent of dust and chaos air. The apartment was a wreck. She picked up a trash bag; the plastic crinkling as she tossed in broken debris. Shadow's muffled howls and frantic scratching were a cacophony that filled the space. Trying to sit, a spring jabbed her backside. Sliding off the couch, she sat on the hard cold floor.

Her mind seemed to crash in on its own thoughts as she weighed what Amara had said. But her own fears, her own mistrusts came rushing back in, reminding her why she didn't trust people.

He'll get bored with me soon. I am just a new plaything that doesn't play well with others, which makes him want me more. I will allow no one to use me again, not after what happened before.

Aris

Chapter 20

Aris squinted at the address on his phone, the screen reflecting in the dark. The name—a cold, stark word—had led him here quickly. A few clicks, a flurry of digital pages, and there she was. Her life illuminated his computer screen. He had poured over the details, going through her social media, her resume, and everything he could find. She wasn't very active on social media, but still there was enough to give him a general picture. There had been three rehab stints before her marriage to a construction worker. She now worked at a small retail store a couple towns over.

He hadn't wanted to tell his parents. He just wanted to see her, the woman who'd given birth to him and then sold him, the chill of that truth settling in his gut like a stone. With no thought of why or how, he just made the drive after the sun went down.

The clock signaled ten o'clock on Saturday night. Flickering porch lights illuminated the house, revealing snapshots of the lives within. He imagined the blonde woman's gentle voice, though he had never heard it. Emerging from his car, he moved in the shadows toward the house. Stopping ten feet from the window, he inhaled, catching the metallic scent of blood mixed with the faint scent of pizza. Two boys, aged eleven and twelve, were chowing down on slices. A brown-haired man entered the living room, his shadow momentarily eclipsing the window as he kissed the woman and tousled the older boy's hair.

"Are we watching a scary movie or a

comedy tonight?" the man asked.

"Scary!" both boys screamed almost in perfect unison.

"That means I get to have Mom cuddle up to me when she gets scared," the man laughed, pulling her down onto the couch.

"Oh, you," she snickered, curling up into his arms.

Is this the life I would have had if she had not sold me? His tumultuous thoughts rumbled. *This is a far cry from the drug addicted mother I had heard about. Is this the life I would have had if she had not sold me? Would she have turned her life around if it weren't for the money?*

He tiptoed around the house; the gravel crunching softly under his feet. Peering through the windows, he saw only framed photographs of the family, their smiles mocking him. A sharp, hollow ache pulsed in his chest as he understood: she likely possessed nothing of him. No photos, no trinkets, just an empty space, a void where memories of the baby boy she'd given away should be. *Does she ever think of me?*

He completed his circuit, returning to the window. Inside, the family's laughter drifted out, unaware of his presence. He focused his will, hoping she would glance his way, acknowledge him, show some sign of her feelings about the boy she'd sold. But her gaze remained fixed on the flickering television screen.

Turning, he walked back to his car, the crunch of gravel a dull sound under his feet. A restlessness filled his soul, with an icy dread settling in his stomach. He took the drive, the road blurring, his mind filled with the images in that picture window. When his tires turned with what felt like their own volition, he real-

183

ized where he had gone. He looked at the apartment complex; the streetlight dappling the perfectly manicured lawn and trees.

Should I go up and knock? His mind churned, toying with the idea. With a shake of his head, he rejected it, tires screeching as he sped from the lot. *Am I a glutton for punishment or what? Why would I waste any more time on a woman who isn't interested in me?*

The drive home was a blur as the miles stretched by. Entering the house, he heard the murmur of voices in the formal living room.

"There he is," Tiberias called out. "Come and greet our guests."

Aris inhaled deeply, suppressing his emotions. He followed the sound, a smirk playing on his lips, a cool glint in his eyes.

Weave Your Dreams, Brew Your Magic in

Rusthollow

Harlow

Chapter 21

Harlow sank to the bare floor, the echo of the empty room amplifying the silence after the movers' departure. A heavy sigh escaped her as she collapsed with a soft thud. *I am going to have to take on more work to pay for the damage.*

Her gaze fixated on the wall by the door. She could almost feel the phantom pressure of his body pressed against hers, a memory both vivid and stinging. A week had passed, a week of expected arrivals that never came. A sob clawed at her throat as she wanted to cry or scream. Her heart was a battlefield, the urge to find him warring with the bitter truth of abandonment. *I pushed him away multiple times. So why would I expect him to show up? He looked so sad when I looked into those green eyes. Why would he want to keep chasing a woman who told him to go away, time and time again? I should be happy he finally did what I said, so why am I sad?*

"I don't want him," she grumbled to herself as she looked away from the wall. The words, crisp and sharp, hung in the air, but even as they escaped her lips, she felt a familiar heat flush her cheeks, betraying the lie's coldness.

She drew her phone, the cool metal a contrast to her clammy hand, seeking escape. The screen glowed, illuminating her face as she scrolled through PixelTome. A picture popped into view, the vibrant colors momentarily stealing her focus. Her breath hitched, a strangled sound in the quiet room, as she desperately tried to figure out what it meant. Alena posted a smiling selfie with a quote that said *Drink what makes you happy with friends who make you smile.* It wasn't so much the quote or the glass of blood that made Harlow pause; it was who was sitting next to her, Aris.

A storm of anger and sadness churned within. She fought to steady herself, but rage consumed her. She leaped up, racing to her closet, dodging Shadow, whose tawny eyes flashed with fury at being disturbed. Inside, she tossed clothes aside, finally grabbing a red bodycon dress. The soft fabric brushed against her skin as she slid it on. Black heels clicked as she stepped into them. In the bathroom, she smoothed on crimson lipstick.

Without a thought, she snatched her purse and keys, then bolted to her car. The engine roared as she drove, parking at Taboos and Voodoos. A cold dread washed over her as she neared the door. *Why am I here? I don't care if he went on a date with a completely vapid, self-absorbed, egotistical vampire.*

Her feet slowed, the cobblestones rough beneath her heels. The line snaked, a vibrant tapestry of scales, fur, and wands shimmering under the streetlamps as magickals lined up. A low growl rumbled from the hulking figure ahead. Then, her gaze fixed on the door. Lucas, a blood witch, his crimson eyes alight, grinned, a flash of white teeth, and beckoned. Her stomach churned as she walked forward, a cold sweat prickling her skin.

"Are you here for some fun, Harlow?" Lucas said as he unhooked the rope to let her in.

Nodding, a smile touched her lips as she realized her voice, trapped, wouldn't emerge. Lucas, rarely seen here, usually worked in the back as a bar back; slinging kegs and cases of beer around was his usual job.

187

"Well, go and enjoy yourself." Lucas laughed, the sound echoing before his face hardened.

Entering the club, her eyes scanned the dim space, catching flashing strobes and bodies pulsing to the heavy bass that vibrated through her chest. The air, thick with the smell of sweat and cheap perfume, pressed close. It didn't take long to find him. She stepped forward, each step faltering. Stopping, a chill of doubt crept in, blurring the edges of her anger. Then, her eyes locked with his. He raised an eyebrow at her. *Too late now, I can't pretend I didn't see him now, and I can't run.*

With shoulders thrown back and head held high, she strode proudly toward the table. Her hands trembled, the last vestiges of her inner confidence dissolving. *He was literally trying to get with me last week, and today he is with her.* She squeezed her eyes shut, willing the anger to resurface, and the familiar heat prickling her skin. *Telling me we have something special, which he probably tells all the girls to get them in bed, then a week later he is with Alena.*

"Well, look what the cat drug in," Aris snorted as he took a sip of his crimson drink.

"Here you are hanging out with someone; I'm sure you have something special with. Does she fight the *feelings* less?"

"She puts up no fight," Aris snickered, rolling his eyes.

"I would never fight my feelings for you, Arie," Alena giggled, putting a possessive hand on his chest.

The fiery rage consumed her, a heat she could feel in her chest as she glared at the hand. She craved to tear it away. Then, Aris's hand moved, and with a swift motion, he removed the offending hand, before

taking another sip.

"You here to meet someone?" Aris snorted.

"No," Harlow grunted. "Just here for a drink, a dance, and not to play games."

"The only one who likes to play games is you." Aris swirled the crimson liquid in his glass. "Always playing hide and seek with those heartstrings."

Alena curled her arm around his arm. "Tell her to leave. We're tired of whatever game the stray is playing."

The two vampires at the booth snickered, a dry, rustling sound. A shared glance, laced with disdain, was cast towards Harlow, the air thickening with unspoken judgment.

"I don't play games like you do," Harlow growled, her temper snapping. "And unlike you." She jabbed a finger towards Aris.

"Little delicacy," he sighed dramatically. "You turned me down on multiple occasions. Am I supposed to just keep chasing you around? I'm done playing cat and mouse with a woman who has shown she's not interested. So, when you are ready to act like an adult and go on an actual date with me, you can ask me; otherwise, I'm done hunting a woman who doesn't know how to follow her own heart."

Her mouth sputtered, a choked sound lost in the din of the club. Turning, she walked away, shoulders slumped. The wind left her sails, leaving a hollow ache where her anger had been.

Johnna Dee

Taboos & Voodoos

Aris

Chapter 22

Aris watched her go, the rhythmic sway of her hips, her shiny, silky brown hair flashing in the strobing lights. He caught the final flicker of sadness in her eyes as she glanced back. *I am such a dick.* He could almost hear the door slam shut over the music, though it was just in his head. *Did she come here to make me feel like shit? Or to find someone new, and I just ruined her night by just being here?* The thought that he might have wrecked her evening brought a flicker of warmth to his chest. A silent, smug comfort bloomed within him.

Alena's touch, a slick slide against his jeans, sent a wave of revulsion through him. He flinched, the fabric of his jeans rough against his skin as he brushed her hand away, his face twisting into a frown.

"I told you we are only friends," he grumbled, tossing back the last of his drink. He felt the blood trickle down his throat as what little pleasure, he found in the evening vanished.

"Oh, poo," Alena purred. "I'm just trying to show you... a good time."

"Yep, this was a totally fun night." Aris snorted sarcastically.

"I don't know why you would be interested in a stray," Alena sighed. She brushed her bleach blonde hair, stiff and smelling faintly of chemicals, off her shoulder causing it swat Aris's face. He clenched his jaw, a physical manifestation of his mounting frustration. "Plus, she is an idiot to turn you down. You are handsome, rich, and come from a good family. What is there to turn down? You know we would make a great couple?"

He furrowed his brow, the strobe lights of the club reflecting across his tense face. As he mentally sifted through options to convey his disinterest gently, each word was a potential landmine, and the pressure of the conversation was a heavy weight.

"Leave the newb alone," Colin laughed. His muddy brown eyes shifted nervously from Aris next to him and Alena. "He needs a break."

"Shush." Alena's hushed command cut through the air. Her hand, a blur, swatted at Colin as her elbow jabbed into Aris's chest, a sudden, jarring impact.

Cammie giggled. "I think Aris should give Alena a *break*."

He heard the murmur of their conversation, a low hum against the clatter of footsteps on the dance floor. The voices faded, unheard. His gaze snapped up, drawn to the flash of pink hair as the waitress neared their table.

"Do you need another round?" the waitress asked.

"Yes, another one for us all," Alena replied.

"Not for me," Aris replied. "I need to get home. My mom has plans." The words hung in the air, thin and unconvincing. Even as the excuse left his lips, the sound of his own voice, flat and weak, confirmed its lameness.

"Oh, you can't leave me alone," Alena grumbled petulantly.

"I'm not leaving you alone; you have Cammie and Colin here with you." His leather wallet emerged, and the crisp rustle of bills filled the air. He flicked a handful of crisp hundreds toward the waitress, a gesture that would easily cover the drinks and provide a hefty tip. "Keep the change."

He gently nudged Alena, the vinyl of the booth squeaking as he rose. He stepped out; the bass throbbing faded, replaced by the cool night air on his skin. Annoyance, a bitter taste, propelled each hurried step away from the club. *I just wanted to get out and relax for one night, for fuck's sake.*

Harlow

Chapter 23

Harlow flung the front door open, its frame groaning in protest, then slammed it shut with a resounding thud that echoed in the silent house. The noise did nothing to soothe the tempest of frustration raging inside. Tears blurred her vision as she'd driven, a dam that had finally burst when she entered the sanctity of her home. Her legs buckled, and she crumpled, sliding down the door to land with a soft thud on the cool hardwood. Knees drawn up, she buried her face.

"Play stupid games and win stupid prizes," she murmured, the words muffled by her arm. The humiliation of the past hour washed over her in a fresh wave. "What was I expecting to happen when I stormed in there like that? Did I think he'd suddenly see past my constant pushing him away? That he'd apologize and everything would magically be fixed?" Her voice, a brittle thread, splintered with a harsh, bitter laugh.

The condescending smirk, a sneer of pure contempt, remained vivid in her mind's eye, its memory igniting fury that battled against the crushing weight of despair. Her head snapped up, the sting of tears still fresh on her cheeks.

I should have known better, she told herself, kicking at the air with a useless foot. I should have just walked away sooner, but my pride, my stubborn, foolish pride, had refused to let me. Now, I am left with nothing but a pounding headache and a heart aching with the weight of my impulsiveness. If I had stayed away from him, it would have been best.

A dark shape loomed, and then a cold, wet nose nudged her foot.

"You think you are so slick, don't you," she murmured. "Do *you* even realize you are half the problem here? I have to work extra hours to fix the destruction you created, or I can just max my credit card out and pray I get enough business to repay it plus interest."

Shadow's tawny eyes, gleaming in the dim light, met hers with a dull, uninterested gaze. Her fingers moved, and she reached over, the rough fur of his head brushing against her skin as she scratched him. "I still love you, though." A soft sigh left her lips.

Her thoughts were in a turbulent swirl as one thought pushed its way to the forefront. *What happens if I give it a try?* Shaking her head, she knew it was nonsense. *We would never work out. He'll get bored; he'll leave. He was already out with another woman tonight.* She told herself repeatedly. But the thought still lingered, digging its claws into her heart.

A mournful mew echoed, thin and reedy, through the still air as Shadow headed towards the kitchen. Following the sound, she went to the cupboard. She reached for a can of food and poured the contents into his ceramic bowl. "What would I lose if I tried?"

Pausing as she set the bowl down. "My pride, my dignity, my heart and most importantly my sanity. But then again, I talk to myself and a werekitty way more than I should."

Pacing the floor, she opened the fridge, the cold air rushing out, and pulled out a dark glass bottle. Ignoring the metallic tang in the air, she tilted it back, the crimson liquid gurgling as she drank. The cool liquid slid down her throat, a stark contrast to her craving. She craved the warm, iron-rich taste of fresh blood, not

the chilled store-bought kind. Sighing, she took another sip, the bottle's cold glass pressing against her lips.

"What do I lose if I don't try?" The words, visible as misty breath, lingered, a silent cloud in the still air, as she wrestled with them.

Aris

Chapter 24

Aris stared, eyes glazed, at the screen's flashing violence. The rapid clicks and whirs of the game filled the silent basement, yet his mind wandered. Since leaving the club, he'd shut off his phone, retreating to the cool, dim gaming room. He'd hoped the game's chaos would drown out his thoughts, but even blasting virtual zombies couldn't silence the worries gnawing at him.

His mother had an interior designer custom-design the room when he was a teen after he expressed interest in gaming. She had hoped he could make friends his own age and invite them here, but most human parents didn't want their children hanging out in a house filled with vampires. So, he had spent many lonely days and nights in his own little cave.

He sank deeper onto the dark brown, soft velvet sectional, feeling its plushness. His feet rested on the cool, smooth dark wood coffee table. The huge television screen flashed with vivid, gory cut scenes, the undead moaning, a chilling sound. He pressed the buttons on his wireless remote. The warm tan walls held framed artwork. Stark black and white comic panels, familiar figures, and dynamic action danced before his eyes. Beside them hung vibrant pieces commissioned from local artists.

"Lambkin," Amara whispered behind him.

The screen flashed, a final image of defeat. The controller clattered on the coffee table. Turning his head, he saw his mother silhouetted in the doorway. "What's up?"

"You haven't slept or eaten since last night," Amara replied, moving into the room.

"Is it really eating if we drink blood?"

"Don't you dare try to change the subject by using that sassy mouth of yours," she growled. "Of course it is eating. I'll have them bring you fresh blood, and then you are going to bed, end of story."

"I'm not tired or hungry then," he shrugged. "I just want to beat this level."

"I know you're lying to me."

"How would you know that?"

"Because I know you," she said, gracefully sitting next to him. Her floral perfume wafted around her gently. "I know when you are sad, which is now."

"I'm not sad, I just want—"

"I will box your ear if you lie to me again," she snorted.

Exhaling a long, shaky breath, he sank back against the plush couch cushions, his head resting on them as his eyes stared at the ceiling. He knew it wasn't his racing heart that betrayed him, but he wondered how she always knew when he wasn't telling the truth. "Humor me and tell me why you think I am sad."

"So, you can get better at hiding your emotions from me? Not going to happen,"

He tilted his head. His eyes, shadowed and unblinking, were a mask of seriousness, reflecting nothing. "Maybe."

She shook her head. "Drink then bed."

He knew he would not sleep, restless anger and frustration churned inside him, a bitter taste on his tongue. He squinted, searching for patience as his clenched fists throbbed, and his barely tamed temper was roaring in his soul. "If I do as I am told, will you answer my question?"

She smiled softly and brushed his hair off his forehead. "I will if you promise to eat and then sleep," she said with a smile, a gentle curve of her lips spreading across her face.

"Fine," he mumbled.

"Your eyes," she whispered, shrugging. "I have stared into those eyes every night since you were born. I can read them like a book."

Closing his eyes, a darkness bloomed. He tilted his head back, a stretch of his neck. A choked laugh clawed at his throat, a scream's echo felt in his chest, but he did neither. "Alright then."

She put her hand on his cheek and turned his face back to look at her. "Harlow is a wounded bird. Wounded birds strike out; they need extra care, understanding, and most of all patience."

Smiling self-deprecatingly, he laughed, "I am not very good at being patient."

"It is because you're young."

"Maybe I am tired of being reminded of my age and tired of chasing a female that insults me at every opportunity."

Sighing, with a wisp of air escaping her lips, his mom rose, the rustle of her skirt the only sound. Her hand paused on the doorknob and turned. "We can

leave age out of this. How about I know more about women, since I am one, than you? Trust me when I say, just be patient. Someone will bring you down a drink if you will. Finish what you are served." The door shut with a quiet click behind her as she left.

The cold glass and the smooth, dark bottle appeared, reflecting the dim light. The clink of the glass against the wooden table echoed softly. A tangy, sweet aroma hinted at the liquid within. "Thanks," he murmured as he heard the door close again.

The clear liquid cascaded into the glass. A familiar, anticipatory wetness coated his mouth as he tilted his head and downed it in a single gulp. He knew the cool drink quelled the growing pangs of the hunger, but his distress had clouded any thought.

He heard the distinct thud of footsteps approaching, the creak of hinges as the door swung inward, revealing a sliver of light. "Thanks for the drink, but I'm not up for another lecture, Mom. Can you not just space them out by, say, twenty-four hours?"

Then he noticed it, a rapid thump that didn't match his mother's steady rhythm. He glanced back and saw her. The dim light silhouetted her form, and his brow furrowed, and there was a tightening in his chest.

Johnna Dee

Damascus

Coven

Harlow

Chapter 25

Harlow watched Aris, his form a stiff silhouette against the bright screen, his back a solid wall. The click-clack of the controller filled the quiet room, a sharp counterpoint to the soft thrum of the game. He remained motionless on the couch, seeming to ignore her. She opened her mouth, and all her frustration word-vomited itself out. "Why would you disrupt my life like you did? Do you think this was something I wanted or was looking for? My quiet life was something I liked. I worked hard for that little bit of peace I had, and then you came in and tossed it into the spin cycle. I have—"

"Whoa," Aris said, raising his hand up.

"As I was saying, I have been–"

"Did you come here to criticize me for chasing after something I know you wanted?" He cut her off again. "Don't worry, I don't want you to have to confront feelings and breach that loneliness you call quiet. I stopped trying. You know where the door is; you can show yourself out."

Her breath, a sharp, silent intake, caught in her throat. The weight of his words settled, heavy and cold. After a tumultuous human life and being turned against her will, she had spent centuries closing herself off against the pain, against the world. Those years led her to a solitary existence. Loneliness, a gnawing emptiness, replaced the familiar ache of fear. She stayed behind the scenes to hide from anything that could hurt her. Safety lay in obscurity, in protection from further hurt. The walls she had built were strong, meant to keep everything out, even love.

Whispering, she murmured, "Maybe I didn't want you to stop trying."

"Maybe I'm tired of playing games."

"Fine, no more games. I'll go on a date with you."

"What was that? Couldn't quite hear you," Aris snorted, returning to his game.

"Don't make me repeat myself, please," she huffed, smoothing down her hair.

"I guess since you don't want to repeat what you said, this convo is over."

The rapid clicks of the controller punctuated the groans of the undead. Blonde hair, illuminated by the screen's glow, bobbed as he hunched over, shoulders tense. The strain in his voice, a low, pained murmur, echoed in the room, a feeling of guilt settling heavy within her.

"Yes, I'll repeat myself," she groaned. "If you'll turn around and at least pretend you're listening."

He tossed the remote, landing with a soft thud against the plush couch. As he stood, the TV's blue glow silhouetted him. His gaze met hers: green eyes, normally warm, were now icy, a chill prickling her skin.

"I said—" she started.

"Again, you need to speak up; the TV is a bit loud."

"You're not going to make this easy, are you?" She huffed.

He cocked an eyebrow. "About as easy as you made it for me."

Her gaze locked onto his eyes, dark pools reflecting an unknown intent, was it a game or was he wanting to hurt her back? A prickle of fear crawled across her skin, the air thick with unspoken tension. The memory of a past happiness, now a faded scent, tugged at her, but the thought of returning to its quiet emptiness felt like a slow, suffocating ache. Raising her voice, she said, "I want to go on a date with you."

He rubbed his hand against his ear as he shook his head. A barely perceptible twitch at the corners of his mouth hinted at a smile. "Are my ears deceiving me? Was that you asking me out or answering a question I didn't ask?"

"Whatever," she growled, rolling her eyes. She took a deep breath, trying to find the courage to finish this conversation. "Will you go out with me?"

His face lit up with a cocky grin. "Well, that's very nice of you to ask. So where were you planning on taking me on this date?"

"Can you just say yes so we can end this conversation?" she grumbled.

"What makes you think I'm gonna say yes?" He winked at her.

Biting her lip, she sank her fangs into the plump flesh before she opened her mouth and spoke. "Well, if your answer is no, then there's no point in my continuing to humiliate myself, is there?" She turned and started towards the door.

The heavy thud echoed as he leaped over the couch. His hand clamped on her arm, the sudden grip a jarring surprise, and spun her around. "I didn't say no

either. I just asked what your plans were for this date."

"Fine," she grumbled. Her mind was a whirlwind of date ideas, but none seemed to stick. "Dinner."

"Just dinner?" he murmured, his voice a low rumble against the quiet. His thumb, warm and rough, traced the curve of her jaw. She felt the familiar heat rise in her cheeks, the sudden, breathless stillness in her chest, and the delicious shivers that danced down her spine.

"Maybe," her husky voice whispered as she shrugged. "A cocktail afterward."

"Your place?" His breath, warm and smelling faintly of blood, fluttered across her face as he moved closer. The soft pad of his thumb gently pressed against her bottom lip.

"Yes." Her voice sounded foreign to her own ears; it was so raspy and husky.

"When is this date you're planning on going to happen?" His voice was feathery soft against her ears as he leaned in.

"Tomorrow," she said, closing her eyes, anticipating the warmth of his kiss, the taste of his mouth.

Then he was gone, having stepped back. "I'll see you tomorrow night when you pick me up then."

She paused, confusion settling in.

"What time are you picking me up?" He smiled, his eyes twinkling with a fiery mirth.

"Huh?"

"Are you changing your mind then?" He raised an eyebrow.

"No!" she shouted. "Fine, tomorrow night I'll pick you up at nine. Why do you always have to be so difficult?"

"Not as difficult as you made it," he smirked. His hand came up and then paused. He tapped her nose. "I'll see you tomorrow."

Weave Your Dreams, Brew Your Magic in

Harlow brushed her hair, the bristles a soft whisper against the strands until they gleamed. Examining her reflection, she used her hands, fingers grazing the silky strands, searching for the perfect style. She gathered her hair into a ponytail, feeling the pull, before releasing it. Then, a bun, secured, then discarded. Frustrated, she turned away from the mirror. *If I don't stop futzing with my appearance I won't leave in time.*

She glanced at the clock; the numbers glaringly bright, a silent command to hurry. Fingers smoothed the turquoise silk of her slip dress, the fabric whispering against her skin, the high slit hinting at the curve of her thigh. She had reviewed every detail of her outfit, with seven changes resulting in this look. Black slingback high heels tapped a staccato rhythm on the wooden floor as she moved. Reaching the door, she grabbed the soft shawl, its familiar weight settling on her shoulders.

Before turning the knob, she turned to Shadow. Scolding him, she said, "Do not break anything else while I'm gone!"

She glared at Shadow, the glint of the lamp reflecting in his tawny eyes as he licked a paw. Then, with a languid stretch, he rubbed the wet paw on the top of his head. His casual pose and the lift of his chin told her he'd follow whatever whim struck him. A soft sigh escaped her as she reached out, the cool metal of the doorknob against her hand, and closed the door gently behind her.

A cool breeze carrying the scent of distant rain, rustled her shawl. She walked to her truck; the gravel crunching underfoot. Then, she stopped. He was there, leaning against her car, a dozen red roses, and a vibrant splash of color in his hand. His black suit, black button-up shirt, and black tie, a stark contrast to the bright flowers, seemed to mold to his form, accentuating his strength. *The suit was probably tailor made for him.*

"Took you long enough to come down here." His voice, a low rumble, filled the air as he closed the space between them. The vibrant crimson petals of the roses brushed against her skin as he handed her the bouquet, their sweet fragrance filling her senses.

She took the flowers, their petals velvety soft. Burying her face in them, she inhaled a sweet, heady perfume, a fragrant whisper filling her lungs. "Aren't I supposed to buy you flowers?"

"Did you?" His eyes were so close she could see the kaleidoscopic of greens in their depths.

"No," she whispered.

A chuckle escaped him as he nodded, a glint in his eyes as his eyes stared at her lips. A single fang pierced her lip as she nibbled.

"You might not be an apple, but I want to sink my teeth into those rosy, red lips of yours, also," his husky voice purred.

His gaze locked with hers. She felt a dizzying sensation, as if falling into a verdant forest. The green of his eyes, like moss-covered trees, held her captive, lost in their shadowy depths.

"Go take care of your flowers so we can go on our date," he smirked.

Nodding, she sprinted back. Inside her apartment, she snatched the nearest vase, its ceramic a contrast to her flushed skin, and, with the gentle splash of water, she filled the vase and arranged the flowers.

Glancing over at Shadow, she saw him eyeing her flowers. "Do not dare touch them! I am serious when I say I will buy you that food you hate for a month if one petal is damaged!"

Returning to her open door, she saw him. He was leaning against the door frame. "Gross food for your kitty?"

"Yes," she nodded.

"Ready?"

"Yes," she giggled.

"I'm glad you like the roses." His smile—a gentle curve of the lips—warmed his face.

His hand met hers, fingers interlacing. She followed, the crunch of gravel underfoot, the scent of damp earth and pine trees fading as he led her to the car. A cool breeze swept across her skin as he opened the door. Inside, the soft hum of music playing as the engine roared to life. They arrived at La Sorcellerie Élevée, a uniformed valet offering a hand as she stepped out.

"I've never eaten here before," she murmured, unsure. *Am I supposed to pay on this date? This place is*

way out of my budget. I am not sure I have enough on my credit card after repairs and furniture. A nervous flutter floated through her stomach.

"I think you'll like it." Aris held out his arm. She slid her hand to rest above his elbow. The soft fabric caressed her palm.

"I'm sure I will," she sighed, mentally thinking about how much money she had available.

The restaurant's warm glow spilled out as they entered. The maître d', a man with slicked-back hair, offered a curt nod, his eyes crinkling slightly. She inhaled, catching the faint scent of ozone in his blood. With a rustle of his perfectly tailored suit, the witch pivoted. Aris trailed behind, the scent of garlic and simmering sauces filling the air. The maître d's heels clicked on the polished floor, barely audible over the hushed murmur of conversations. Her gaze flickered to Aris, a silent question in her eyes. *Was he here so often that they didn't need words?* As she turned, the crisp white tablecloth beckoned, but no menu remained on the table.

"He forgot to leave the menu," Harlow whispered.

"Everything has been taken care of," Aris said with a smirk.

"What do you mean, taken care of?" Her voice, a melodic ripple, questioned as her gaze swept the room, eyes widening, taking in the details of the surroundings. She saw the magickals filling the tables, their attire shimmering, fabrics rustling softly, a fortune in clothes that probably cost more than her yearly wage. Sparkling chandeliers cast a warm, gentle glow. The clink of silverware was barely audible as waiters moved soundlessly.

"I mean, I planned everything. So, all you need to do is sit back and relax." A warm smile spread across his face.

"So, you even chose what blood I'll have?" A flicker of irritation, a quick, hot prickling under her skin, like a sudden, unwelcome breeze.

"If you want, I can cancel everything, and you can choose where to go," he paused. "But you'll miss out on a wonderful meal."

She mulled over his words, her eyes drifting across the restaurant again. The smells wafting—food, blood pumping, and champagne—around her smelled delicious, and she was hungry. "Fine, we can stay. But next time I would like a say in what we drink."

"So, you've decided there will be a next time?"

Her eyes flickered, drawn to the sculpted blonde brow, a crimson tide washing over her cheeks.

"Maybe." She shrugged.

"Don't try playing hard to get too long, I'm already bored of it."

With a frustrated huff, her eyes, now rolling, caught the glint of the harsh overhead light. "Fine, there will be a second date."

"And a third?"

"Only if you behave."

"How should I behave?"

She glared at him as a waiter, his movements crisp, poured a crimson liquid, glinting in the dim light, into the glass. She lifted the cool glass, the warm nectar, smelling faintly of iron, sliding smoothly down her

throat, a rich taste that was far superior to what she had gotten from Onyx, almost like fresh blood. Closing her eyes, she savored the sensation.

"Gods, you even make drinking look sexy," his husky voice purred.

She opened her eyes, a warmth blossomed on her pale skin, a creeping blush spreading like a sudden, unwanted sunrise. "Umm," she hummed. "Thank you."

"Food should be here soon," he murmured.

"Food?" she asked, shocked.

"Yes, food."

Her eyes gleamed with a quizzical glint. The waiter arrived as he was setting down two plates. The raw meat glistened, blood pooling around it. She inhaled, the scent of capers and lemon filling her nostrils.

"What is this?" she murmured.

He set his fork down and smiled at her tenderly. "Steak Tartare."

"Oh," she mumbled.

Her fork pierced the tender meat, and she lifted it, the juices glistening. Eyes closed, a wave of flavor washed over her, dissolving on her tongue. A faint clink echoed, and she opened her eyes to the waiter replenishing her glass with a crimson stream.

"I never knew they served food we could eat here," she whispered, scooping up another bite of food.

"There are few things we can eat, but they have found a way to serve something on the menu for almost every type of magical creature, including us."

"It's delicious." Her taste buds sang with the savory flavors. Could she capture this culinary magic by finding the recipe and making it at home?

"So, are we going to talk about our feelings?"

"If you want." Her smile, a hesitant curve, barely touched her lips. A tight knot twisted in her stomach, churning the remains of her meal with a queasy lurch.

"I want to be with you and only you." His voice, a low rumble that vibrated in the air, was firm and confident as his gaze locked onto hers, the intensity of his stare a tangible heat.

The knot in her stomach loosened, a subtle shift she felt as his words echoed in her ears. Her lips parted, but a familiar fear clamped them shut. The warm glass of her drink met her lips as she swallowed a large gulp. Finally, she opened her mouth, and the words tumbled out, "I want to be with you, but..."

He looked at her, eyes steady and unwavering, a quiet stillness hanging between them.

She longed to speak, but the words, like shadows, clung to the back of her throat. She felt the weight of unspoken fears pressing down, and a desperate urge to conceal them, to keep them hidden from any judging eyes. A lone sentence, barely audible, escaped her lips. "I'm scared."

He nodded slowly, the dim light glinting off his glass as he finished his drink with a gulp. Without a word, she pushed herself up, the soft fabric of her skirt brushing against her legs and bolted to the bathroom. Her heart hammered against her ribs, a frantic drumbeat in her ears as the familiar dread washed over her. She leaned against the cold metal stall door, shutting her eyes.

Harlow

Chapter 26

Harlow sighed, a gust of air escaping her lips. Fear weighed her down like a heavy cloak. Cool wood met her fingertips as she touched the stall door. Leaning her forehead on it, she tried to ground herself. The stall—a tiny room in itself—enveloped her. Dark navy and gold stripes went up and down the walls. The oak door, reaching the floor, offered easy concealment.

The click echoed, the bathroom door swinging open, and she tensed. Soft footsteps whispered across the tile, ceasing near her stall, followed by gentle rapping.

"It's occupied," she murmured.

"I know. Open the door."

She opened the door and stared into Aris's green eyes. "What if someone comes in and sees you in the woman's bathroom?"

Her knees hit the rim of the toilet as he nudged her in. His shadow fell over her as he stepped inside. The door slammed shut, the latch clicking with a metallic finality. "They won't realize."

"Of course they will."

"No, they won't. Let's have a private conversation here where no one else is." She opened her mouth to respond, but he held his hand up. "I know no one else is around because the only hearts I hear are yours and mine."

She tried to think of a reason to avoid this conversation, but could not find one, so she nodded.

His calloused fingers gently swept the silken strands of hair away from her flushed cheek. "Over time, I'll show you that you have nothing to fear. Whenever you're ready, you can tell me your secrets. I am here, and I am patient."

She rested her head on his chest, listening to the soft thunder of its beat. His hand, large and calloused, ascended and made slow circles on her back, the friction a warm whisper against the thin fabric of her dress.

"Are you willing to give us a chance?" His voice, a mere whisper, brushed against her ears, and the tremor within it hinted at a vulnerability that she could almost feel in the flutter in her chest.

She nodded, her cheek brushing against the soft fabric of his shirt, the scent of his cologne and a hint of soap filling her nostrils.

"Can you say the words?" His hand slid up and cupped her chin, tilting her head up to meet his gaze.

She stared into his eyes, breathing, "Yes."

His mouth claimed hers, a hot pressure. A wet swirl of tongues ignited a tempest within her. Twisting, he pinned her against the cool bathroom stall wall. His hard body, a burning brand, met hers. A hand, rough against her, found the silk of her dress, sliding it up. Then, fingers, a tantalizing dance of sensation, brushed her skin, tracing a path along her thigh as they lifted the skirt.

Her laughter, light and airy, bounced off the walls. Her hands, small and delicate, strained against his chest. He stood firm, a solid, unyielding wall against her attempts. "Stop!" she whispered urgently. "What if

someone walks in here?”

“No one will walk in,” he stated matter-of-factly.

“How do you know?” She rolled her eyes. A soft, insistent pressure began working its way beneath the flimsy silk of her thong, his fingers whispering against her skin. She swatted at it, a delicate gesture. “Behave! We are in a busy restaurant.”

“We are completely alone and—”

“For now!”

His hand rose as the rough pad of his forefinger met the soft warmth of her lips. “Shhh.”

“We are completely alone, and I want to show you how much I will cherish you starting now.” His voice, a low murmur, vibrated in the sudden silence. A hand, warm and insistent, found the delicate silk of her panties. Fabric tore with a sharp, definitive rip.

“Aris,” she gasped.

“Someone might hear you,” he murmured, pressing his lips against hers.

His tongue plunged into her mouth, a forceful invasion that swiftly overcame her resistance. She tasted the savory meal, the metallic tang of blood, and yearned for more of him. Her hands ascended, encircling his neck. Fingers wove through his silky hair as tongues clashed. Strong fingers gripped her flesh, pulling her closer. She felt his hard shaft, cloaked in the soft fabric of his pants, pressed against her stomach before he lifted her hips and pressed that hardness against her core.

His lips peeled away, then his mouth traced a path down her neck. A soft thud echoed as he knelt. His hands found her inner thighs, skin warm against

hers, gently widening the space. A flick of his tongue on her clit drew a sharp inhale. A thumb slid inside; her hips arched, pressing closer to his face. Out came a soft groan. His thumb pulsed in and out while his mouth closed around her, drawing her deeper. Her core clenched, breathe catching.

A soft creak echoed. Her fingers clutched his hair, tilting his head down, pressing it back into her center. He shrugged, then his lips and thumb resumed their rhythm. Her breath hitched, a ragged gasp escaping. A soft chuckle and the slam of a door. Shame flickered, but his wet tongue and skilled hand banished every thought.

Her head tilted back, her gaze fixed on the stark white ceiling. As his tongue danced across her clit, her eyes fluttered closed. Her fingers tangled in his hair, her core clenching. A storm brewed within her with each lick, each touch. Then, a pause. Her eyes snapped open as she saw him stand. His pants parted, revealing his shaft. Her hand found it, caressing it up and down, his soft moan filling the air.

"Did you hear that?" a random woman asked.

"Hear what?" another woman sighed. Splashing water echoed, filling the space.

Her hand stilled, and she inhaled sharply, holding her breath. His forehead pressed against hers. He clasped her wrist, tugging it from his flesh. She let go, barely breathing. His hand found her ass, lifting her leg. She shook her head, meeting eyes now clouded with desire. The glint in his eyes—a warm, hard light—mirrored the hard upward curl of his lips. His fingers met the smooth, yielding skin of her leg. He hoisted it up, sliding it up the striped wall.

"I guess it was nothing," the first woman laughed.

"I ate so much," the second woman said. "I don't think I'll eat for a week after this."

Laughter, bright and tinkling, spilled from the other side of the door, a stark contrast to the heat building between them. His rigid length pulsed, a heavy drumbeat against her. She shook her head, a desperate plea unspoken, but his thrust was relentless, a slow, burning invasion inch by agonizingly slow inch as he penetrated her.

"I am so glad the boys brought us here on our double date," the first woman said.

The world narrowed as he pressed, one slow thrust, and he filled her up. Her breath hitched, a silent gasp against the pressure, and she clamped down, fangs sinking into her lip to trap the sound.

"I can't believe we are actually on a double date with the hottest boys at Moonrise," one giggled.

He withdrew his shaft, her nails, sharp against his skin, dug into the muscles of his shoulders.

"The hottest twins!" the other exclaimed. "We are the luckiest witches!"

He thrust inside, driving deep. Her body shook as he nipped her neck. His fangs grazed her skin. Her heart hammered, a frantic rhythm threatening to fill the room so everyone would be able to hear it.

"Okay," one said. "I am ready to go back to our handsome dates."

He withdrew, his tip grazing her entrance. Heels tapped, then the door yielded, then slammed. With a forceful lunge, he plunged deeper. No longer hushed, his motions quickened. Her fingers tangled in his hair, head tilting, fangs sinking into his neck. Warm nec-

tar flooded her mouth. Elbows hooked on her knees; he lifted her other leg up. His rhythm quickened. His ragged breaths rasped near her ear, the scent of blood filling her nostrils as she withdrew her fangs.

His fangs pierced her skin, a burning pleasure as he drank of her nectar. Her legs locked around his waist, burying him deeper, nails digging into his scalp. His right hand found her bundle of nerves, thumb circling. She clawed at his hair as the heat intensified. His thumb quickened, mirroring the beat of each plunge. Her core tightened as the storm threatened to consume her.

Her legs trembled, a visible tremor running through them. Her hands quivered, fingers twitching. The storm within swelled, a silent, powerful force. Every nerve thrummed, a symphony of sensation. Her body grew taut, muscles clenched, before exploding in a wave of pure pleasure. Her body rocked, waves of ecstasy washing over her.

Her body sagged, heavy against him as he pinned her to the cool, rough wall. "We should leave before..." she breathed, her voice barely audible, before the soft creak of the door sliced through the tense silence.

His nose nudged her neck, the rough stubble a faint scratch. Silence hung thick, save for their racing hearts. She gripped his shirt, muscles taut, terrified of a whisper as a person shuffled around. Then, the click of the door as it closed shut, and a rush of released breath filled the air.

"We should leave before someone else walks in here," she breathed, pushing his shoulder. Her legs slid down his waist. The soft scrape of fabric against skin accompanied the motion, and then her feet found the solid, cool earth.

"If you insist," he murmured, pressing a gentle kiss on her lips.

"You are incorrigible." She rolled her eyes as she ran her fingers through his hair, smoothing it out as best she could.

"Always," he smirked. "You have always been in my thoughts since the first moment I met you."

"Wha... Wha... What?" Her voice, a shaky tremor, escaped her lips as a lightness bloomed in her chest, a sensation she hadn't known she was missing.

"I said I can't stop thinking about you."

"Oh," she said in a breathless whisper. Smoothing the silk against her skin, she felt the cool fabric. Her gaze snagged on the ripped thong, a splash of black against the grey marble floors.

"That's all you have to say?" he whispered as he zipped his pants up.

"No," she said, chewing on lip. "It's hard to let people in, but I let you in, even when I didn't want to."

"So, have I wiggled my way into that sweet little heart of yours?" He gently tapped her heart before pulling her into his arms.

Pressing her head into his shoulder, she inhaled the familiar scent of his cologne, searching for the words to explain the warring thoughts and emotions. Closing her eyes, she felt a comforting warmth bloom in her soul. "You did."

"Before you I felt so restless, unsure about my life," he murmured into her hair. "I just felt like I was floating. Then I met you, and I knew what I wanted in life, and it was you"

A smile spread across her face as her eyes beamed with joy. "It's hard to open up, to say how I feel, and I can't believe I am going to say it in a bathroom at a fancy restaurant, but I've missed you these last few days."

"It doesn't matter where we are as long as we are together." He stroked her hair comfortingly.

"But for how long?" she whispered, barely audible to her own ears.

"Forever if you quit fighting how much we love each other." His hand fisted in her hair and gently tugged her head backward. Her eyes locked with his, and he smiled softly. "I knew from the moment I saw you, and today I know the truth even more. I love you. So can you quit fighting me and just accept how you feel for me?"

"What makes you think I have some profoundly deep feelings for you?" she said, noticing a flicker of insecurity flash in those eyes. Sighing, she felt the fight leave her like a balloon deflating. "Fine, I have feelings for you."

His hand released its grip on her hair, his brow creasing as he raised an eyebrow.

Exhaling deeply, she closed her eyes before opening them again. "Why do you push so hard?"

"Some things are worth pushing to get."

Her gaze locked onto forest-green eyes, searching for answers. A battle raged within; one part wanted to resist, the other, to surrender. Fear lingered as she felt herself drawn in. Seeing his vulnerability, she knew she could no longer resist. *Do I even want to fight?* She

mulled over the question, realizing she didn't.

"You're right," she murmured. "I..." The words lodged in her throat as she tried to remember the last time she had said those words. No memories came back to her. Swallowing the lump, she closed her eyes, no longer able to meet his gaze. "I... I love you, too." Her voice was so soft she didn't know if he even heard her.

Laughing, he squeezed her tight. "That will do for now. Maybe one day you'll be brave enough to say it louder than a mouse's squeak, little delicacy."

"I am brave, and I said it louder than a mouse," she huffed, rolling her eyes.

"Sure, you did." He squeezed her tight. "For my own ego, were you jealous when you ran into us at the club? Just so you know. I was never interested in Alena, by the way. She drove me nuts."

"I will not feed your over-inflated ego!" she laughed, punching his chest softly. "We should leave the bathroom before someone else comes in."

She playfully shoved him, the impact a soft thud. He released her, and her hand shot out, fingers finding his. They walked, hands clasped, out of the bathroom.

He tugged her close; his breath, warm and scented with the fresh taste of blood and her, tickled her ear as he whispered, "You taste better than anything they serve on the menu."

Recipes

Giggamon Bun

Ingredients

Cinnamon Roll Dough

- 4 1/2 – 5 cups all-purpose flour
- 1/3 cup granulated sugar
- 2 packets Yeast (about 4 1/2 tsp)
- 1 tsp salt
- 1 1/2 cups water
- 6 tbsp unsalted butter
- 1 large egg

Filling

- 1/4 cup unsalted butter, room temp
- 1/2 cup light brown sugar, packed
- 1 tbsp cinnamon

Cream Cheese Icing

- 4 oz cream cheese, room temp
- 1/4 cup unsalted butter, room temp
- 1 cup powdered sugar
- 2 tsp vanilla extract

Instructions

Cinnamon Roll Dough

1. In a large mixing bowl, mix together 2 cups of flour, sugar, yeast, and salt.
2. In a heat-safe bowl, combine the water and butter (cut into tbsp size tabs). Heat in the microwave for 30 sec—45 sec. The butter should not be melted completely, just soft.
3. Pour the wet ingredients into the dry ingredients along with the egg and mix with a wooden spoon.
4. **Optional:** Time for the spell, turn the wooden spoon three times counterclockwise while reciting the incantation. Then repeat the steps, turning the spoon in a clockwise motion. The above steps three times while reciting the spell.
   a. **Spell:** "May the Goddess of Light and the God of Laughter bring forth a round of giggles by the turn of my spoon, and flick of my wrist. With light and laughter, I bring forth this wish upon thee."
5. Add 2 more cups of flour and mix. It should turn pretty thick and sticky at this point.
6. Add in 1/2 cup of flour and mix again. It should now be difficult to stir. Once it reaches that point, set the spoon to the side and use your hands to knead the dough.
7. Add another 1/4 cup of flour and continue to mix and knead by hand. It should be smooth, soft and tacky. With a clean finger, press it into the dough. If your finger is sticking, add another 1/4 cup of flour and knead again. If it's not, then shape it into a ball and let it rest uncovered for 10 minutes
8. When the 10 minutes are up, the dough should have puffed up quite a bit, not quite doubled in

size.

9. Place the dough on a lightly floured surface and pat it into a rough rectangle shape. Using a rolling pin roll it out into a 10×15 inch rectangle.

10. Spread the room-temperature butter (from filling) into a thin and even layer, leaving about 1/2-inch border all around the outside of the dough. Sprinkle it with brown sugar and spread it evenly with your hand. Then top it with cinnamon.

11. Working from the longer end of the dough, roll it up into a log. Place your hands at each end of the log and give it a gentle squeeze to compact the log of dough, sometimes it stretches out during the rolling process.

12. Using the floss, slide it under the roll and toss both ends of the floss over top. Pull them through to create a cut. Cut off the two ends of the log and then cut the rest into 12 pieces.

    a. Cut the rolls with unflavored dental floss for the best outcome. If you don't have floss, a thin sewing thread might also work. When you use a knife, slowly sawing back and forth and be careful not to press directly into the rolls, this might deform them, making them more oval.

    b. Cut the entire log in half, then cut those two halves in half to create 4 segments. Cut each of the four segments into 3 rolls to get 12.

13. Place the rolls in a buttered or greased 9×13 inch dish (you could also use two 9 inch round pans, dividing in half). It doesn't matter if the rolls are touching.

14. Put it somewhere warm and drape a towel over it, allowing it to rise for an hour. For those living in colder climates, preheating the oven to the lowest temperature. After it's warmed up, turn off the oven and put the rolls inside. This pro-

vides a warm atmosphere that encourages the rolls to proof.

15. Preheat the oven to 350F after they have proofed. They should have doubled in size.
16. Bake for 25-30 minutes or until the tops are light golden brown. While they cool, make the icing.

Cream Cheese Icing

1. Make sure the cream cheese and butter are at room temperature; otherwise, the icing will be lumpy. Combine them in a bowl, mashing with a fork.
2. Add the vanilla and powdered sugar and then mash once more with the fork. As the mixture loosens, switch to a whisk and mix until smooth.
3. Spread onto the warm rolls.

Devil's Food Cheer Cake

Ingredients

For the Chocolate Cake

- 1 1/2 cups self-rising flour
- 1 tsp baking soda
- 1 cup cocoa powder
- 1/2 tsp salt
- 1 cup caster sugar
- 1 cup brown sugar, lightly packed
- 1/2 cup boiling water
- 1 tsp instant coffee granules
- 1 cup canola oil
- 1 cup milk
- 2 eggs
- 1 tbsp white vinegar
- 1 tsp vanilla

For the Whipped Chocolate Ganache

- 1 cup heavy whipping cream
- 14 oz block of dark or semi-sweet chocolate, roughly chopped
- 1/2 cup icing sugar/confectioner's sugar

Instructions

For the Chocolate Cake

1. Preheat the oven to 320F. Grease and line two 8-inch round cake tins with baking paper.

2. Combine the flour, baking soda, cocoa powder, and salt in a large mixing bowl by sifting. Mix in the sugar.
3. In a separate medium mixing bowl, whisk together boiling water and instant coffee powder until the coffee granules dissolve. Whisk in canola oil, milk, eggs, vinegar and vanilla essence.
4. **Optional**: Time for the spell, turn the wooden spoon three times counterclockwise while reciting the incantation. Then repeat the steps, turning the spoon in a clockwise motion. The above steps three times while reciting the spell.
   a. **Spell**: "Love and warmth fill thy soul. Sadness and fear begone, and plight be mild. May you open yourself and let the cheer flow in. With light and laughter, I bring forth this wish upon thee."
5. Create a well in the middle of the dry ingredients. Pour in the wet ingredients. Combine until the mixture is uniform. Some lumps are acceptable.
6. Distribute the batter equally into the prepared tins. Bake for 45-50 minutes, or until a skewer shows a few moist crumbs. Leave the cakes in the tins to cool for 10 minutes, then move to a rack.

For the Whipped Chocolate Ganache

1. Heat the cream in a medium, heat-safe bowl on high for 90 seconds or until bubbles form.
2. Incorporate the chopped chocolate and let it sit for 5 minutes.
3. Mix until the chocolate melts completely. If the chocolate isn't melting, microwave the ganache in short 10-second bursts, stirring between, until smooth. Set the ganache aside to cool for half an

hour.
4. Put the ganache in the large bowl of a stand mixer with the whisk on. Whip at top speed for 8-10 minutes, or until the ganache is light, fluffy, and holds a soft peak.
5. Sift icing sugar, then whisk for two more minutes or until firmer. Wait to assemble the cake until the ganache is at room temperature. Beat the ganache for 30 seconds to soften it if it's too hard.

To Assemble

1. Place the cooled cake onto a large platter or serving board. Top the first cake with a quarter of the ganache frosting. Use a palette knife or flat-bladed knife to smooth over the cake.
2. Put the second cake on top of the first, inverted. Use half of the remaining ganache to top it. Cover the cake with a thick layer of ganache and smooth the edges.
3. Spread a thick layer of ganache on the cake sides and smooth it with a knife. Keep the cake refrigerated until serving. The ganache will become firmer in the next couple of hours.

Clarity Tea Latte with Ice

Ingredients:

- 1 tsp ginkgo biloba leaves
- 1/2 tsp gotu kola leaves
- 1/4 tsp rose petals
- 1 cup boiling water
- Tea ball or bag (for putting leaves in)
- ½ cup frothed milk
- Ice (optional)

Directions:

1. Put the dry ingredients in a tea ball or bag.
2. Allow the tea to steep for 1-4 minutes in boiling water.
3. **Optional**: Recite the spell while stirring clockwise 3 times and then counterclockwise 3 times.
   a. **Spell:** "I call on the Goddess to ask for help. Remove the block that is before the ones that drink this. Break the block so they can see with clarity. I chant these words for clearness of sight. So, mote it be."
4. Allow to cool. Pour over ice (optional). Top off with the frothed milk.

ABOUT THE AUTHOR

Thank you for taking the time to read this story by author Johnna Dee. She is a fantasy romance writer who has three series out at the time of publication. Initially, her creative journey began with poetry, where she honed her skills in crafting evocative and lyrical verses. As her passion for storytelling grew, she ventured into the realm of novels, weaving intricate plots and enchanting worlds that transport readers to extraordinary realms.

For more exclusive content and other goodies, sign-up for Johnna Dee's newsletter **https://linktr.ee/johnnadee** or check out her website **https://alstroemeriapub.com/**.

ALSO BY THE AUTHOR

Ascelin Series:

Crest of the Fallen

Crest of the Scorned

Crest of the Forgotten

Gorgo Series:

Betrayal of the Gorgon

Ransom of the Gorgon

Immortality of the Gorgon (February 2026)

Hogsmead Series:

Shifting Sides

Shifting Lines (June 2026)

Magickal Morsels Series:

Cake with a Slice of Vengeance

Cake it Easy

Cake it or Leave it (October 2026)

Standalone Books:

The Darkside of Midnight

Lies Among Gods (June 2026)

Calpa Series

Co-written with Fleur DeVillainy:

The Clan of Mist

The Clan of Deception

The Clan of Luna (coming 2026)

Email
SIGN UP